Thomas Bailey Aldrich

The Poems of Thomas Bailey Aldrich

Thomas Bailey Aldrich

The Poems of Thomas Bailey Aldrich

ISBN/EAN: 9783744714419

Printed in Europe, USA, Canada, Australia, Japan

Cover: Foto ©Andreas Hilbeck / pixelio.de

More available books at **www.hansebooks.com**

THE POEMS

OF

THOMAS BAILEY ALDRICH

ILLUSTRATED

BY

THE PAINT AND CLAY CLUB

BOSTON
HOUGHTON, MIFFLIN AND COMPANY
New York: 11 East Seventeenth Street
The Riverside Press, Cambridge
1882

The Riverside Press, Cambridge:
Electrotyped and Printed by H. O. Houghton & Co.

CONTENTS.

III.

SPRING IN NEW ENGLAND AND OTHER POEMS.

IV.

FRIAR JEROME'S BEAUTIFUL BOOK, ETC.

V.

SONNETS.

LIST OF ILLUSTRATIONS.

The engravers are: GEORGE F. ANDREW, W. B. CLOSSON, W. J. DANA, J. P. DAVIS, FRANK FRENCH, ARTHUR HAYMAN, *and* S. L. PUTNAM.

FLOWER AND THORN.

FLOWER AND THORN.

I.

At Shiraz, in a sultan's garden, stood
  A tree whereon a curious apple grew,
  One side like honey, and one side like rue.

Thus sweet and bitter is the life of man,
  The sultan said, for thus together grow
  Bitter and sweet, but wherefore none may know.

Herewith together you have flower and thorn.
  Both rose and brier, for thus together grow
  Bitter and sweet, but wherefore none may know.

II.

Take them and keep them,
Silvery thorn and flower,
Plucked just at random
In the rosy weather —
Snowdrops and pansies,
Sprigs of wayside heather,
And five-leaved wild-rose
Dead within an hour.

Take them and keep them:
Who can tell? some day, dear,
(Though they be withered,
Flower and thorn and blossom,)
Held for an instant
Up against thy bosom,
They might make December
Seem to thee like May, dear!

1.

CLOTH OF GOLD.

CLOTH OF GOLD.

PROEM.

You ask us if by rule or no
Our many-colored songs are wrought:
Upon the cunning loom of thought,
We weave our fancies, so and so.

2

The busy shuttle comes and goes
Across the rhymes, and deftly weaves
A tissue out of autumn leaves,
With here a thistle, there a rose.

With art and patience thus is made
The poet's perfect Cloth of Gold:
When woven so, nor moth nor mould
Nor time can make its colors fade.

A TURKISH LEGEND.

A CERTAIN Pasha, dead these thousand years,
Once from his harem fled in sudden tears,

And had this sentence on the city's gate
Deeply engraven, "Only God is great."

So those four words above the city's noise
Hung like the accents of an angel's voice,

And evermore, from the high barbacan,
Saluted each returning caravan.

Lost is that city's glory. Every gust
Lifts, with crisp leaves, the unknown Pasha's dust.

And all is ruin — save one wrinkled gate
Whereon is written, "Only God is great."

AN ARAB WELCOME.

BECAUSE thou com'st, a weary guest,
Unto my tent, I bid thee rest.
This cruse of oil, this skin of wine,
These tamarinds and dates are thine;
And while thou eatest, Medjid, there,
Shall bathe the heated nostrils of thy mare.

Illah il' Allah! Even so
An Arab chieftain treats a foe,
Holds him as one without a fault
Who breaks his bread and tastes his salt;
And, in fair battle, strikes him dead
With the same pleasure that he gives him bread!

THE CRESCENT AND THE CROSS.

Kind was my friend who, in the Eastern land,
Remembered me with such a gracious hand,
And sent this Moorish Crescent which has been
Worn on the haughty bosom of a queen.

No more it sinks and rises in unrest
To the soft music of her heathen breast;
No barbarous chief shall bow before it more,
No turbaned slave shall envy and adore.

I place beside this relic of the Sun
A Cross of Cedar brought from Lebanon,
Once borne, perchance, by some pale monk who trod
The desert to Jerusalem — and his God.

Here do they lie, two symbols of two creeds,
Each meaning something to our human needs,
Both stained with blood, and sacred made by faith,
By tears, and prayers, and martyrdom, and death.

That for the Moslem is, but this for me!
The waning Crescent lacks divinity:
It gives me dreams of battles, and the woes
Of women shut in dim seraglios.

But when this Cross of simple wood I see,
The Star of Bethlehem shines again for me,
And glorious visions break upon my gloom —
The patient Christ, and Mary at the Tomb!

THE UNFORGIVEN.

NEAR my bed, there, hangs the picture jewels could
    not buy from me :
'T is a Siren, a brown Siren, in her sea-weed dra-
    pery,
Playing on a lute of amber, by the margin of a
    sea.

In the east, the rose of morning seems as if 't would
    blossom soon,
But it never, never blossoms, in this picture ; and the
    moon
Never ceases to be crescent, and the June is always
    June.

And the heavy-branched banana never yields its
    creamy fruit ;
In the citron-trees are nightingales forever stricken
    mute ;
And the Siren sits, her fingers on the pulses of the
    lute.

In the hushes of the midnight, when the heliotropes
    grow strong

With the dampness, I hear music — hear a quiet,
    plaintive song —
A most sad, melodious utterance, as of some immor-
    tal wrong —

Like the pleading, oft repeated, of a Soul that pleads
    in vain,
Of a damnéd Soul repentant, that would fain be pure
    again! —
And I lie awake and listen to the music of her pain.

And whence comes this mournful music? — whence,
    unless it chance to be
From the Siren, the brown Siren, in her sea-weed
    drapery,
Playing on a lute of amber, by the margin of a sea.

DRESSING THE BRIDE.

A FRAGMENT.

So, after bath, the slave-girls brought
The broidered raiment for her wear,
The misty izar from Mosul,
The pearls and opals for her hair,

The slippers for her supple feet,
(Two radiant crescent moons they were,)
And lavender, and spikenard sweet,
And attars, nedd, and richest musk.
When they had finished dressing her,
(The eye of morn, the heart's desire!)
Like one pale star against the dusk,
A single diamond on her brow
Trembled with its imprisoned fire!

TWO SONGS FROM THE PERSIAN.

I.

O CEASE, sweet music, let us rest!
Too soon the hateful light is born;
Henceforth let day be counted night,
And midnight called the morn.

O cease, sweet music, let us rest!
A tearful, languid spirit lies,
Like the dim scent in violets,
In beauty's gentle eyes.

There is a sadness in sweet sound
That quickens tears. O music, lest
We weep with thy strange sorrow, cease!
Be still, and let us rest.

II.

Ah! sad are they who know not love,
But, far from passion's tears and smiles,
Drift down a moonless sea, beyond
The silvery coasts of fairy isles.

And sadder they whose longing lips
Kiss empty air, and never touch
The dear warm mouth of those they love —
Waiting, wasting, suffering much.

But clear as amber, fine as musk,
Is life to those who, pilgrim-wise,
Move hand in hand from dawn to dusk,
Each morning nearer Paradise.

O, not for them shall angels pray!
They stand in everlasting light,
They walk in Allah's smile by day,
And nestle in his heart by night.

TIGER-LILIES.

I LIKE not lady-slippers,
Nor yet the sweet-pea blossoms,
Nor yet the flaky roses,
    Red, or white as snow;
I like the chaliced lilies,
The heavy Eastern lilies,
The gorgeous tiger-lilies,
    That in our garden grow!

For they are tall and slender;
Their mouths are dashed with carmine;
And when the wind sweeps by them,
    On their emerald stalks
They bend so proud and graceful —
They are Circassian women,
The favorites of the Sultan,
    Adown our garden walks!

And when the rain is falling,
I sit beside the window
And watch them glow and glisten,
    How they burn and glow!
O for the burning lilies,
The tender Eastern lilies,
The gorgeous tiger-lilies,
    That in our garden grow!

THE SULTANA.

In the draperies' purple gloom,
In the gilded chamber she stands,
I catch a glimpse of her bosom's bloom,
And the white of her jewelled hands.

Each wandering wind that blows
By the lattice, seems to bear
From her parted lips the scent of the rose,
And the jasmine from her hair.

Her dark-browed odalisques lean
To the fountain's feathery rain,
And a paroquet, by the broidered screen,
Dangles its silvery chain.

But pallid, luminous, cold,
Like a phantom she fills the place,
Sick to the heart, in that cage of gold,
With her sumptuous disgrace!

THE WORLD'S WAY.

At Haroun's court it chanced, upon a time,
An Arab poet made this pleasant rhyme:

" The new moon is a horseshoe, wrought of God,
Wherewith the Sultan's stallion shall be shod."

On hearing this, his highness smiled, and gave
The man a gold-piece. *Sing again, O slave!*

Above his lute the happy singer bent,
And turned another gracious compliment.

And, as before, the smiling Sultan gave
The man a sekkah. *Sing again, O slave!*

Again the verse came, fluent as a rill
That wanders, silver-footed, down a hill.

The Sultan, listening, nodded as before,
Still gave the gold, and still demanded more.

The nimble fancy that had climbed so high
Grew weary with its climbing by and by:

Strange discords rose; the sense went quite amiss;
The singer's rhymes refused to meet and kiss:

Invention flagged, the lute had got unstrung,
And twice he sang the song already sung.

The Sultan, furious, called a mute, and said,
O Musta, straightway whip me off his head!

Poets! not in Arabia alone
You get beheaded when your skill is gone.

LATAKIA.

I.

When all the panes are hung with frost,
Wild wizard-work of silver lace,
I draw my sofa on the rug
Before the ancient chimney-place.
Upon the painted tiles are mosques
And minarets, and here and there
A blind muezzin lifts his hands
And calls the faithful unto prayer.
Folded in idle, twilight dreams,
I hear the hemlock chirp and sing
As if within its ruddy core
It held the happy heart of Spring.
Ferdousi never sang like that,
Nor Saadi grave, nor Hafiz gay:

I lounge, and blow white rings of smoke,
And watch them rise and float away.

II.

The curling wreaths like turbans seem
Of silent slaves that come and go —
Or Viziers, packed with craft and crime,
Whom I behead from time to time,
With pipe-stem, at a single blow.

And now and then a lingering cloud
Takes gracious form at my desire,
And at my side my lady stands,
Unwinds her veil with snowy hands —
A shadowy shape, a breath of fire!

O Love, if you were only here
Beside me in this mellow light,
Though all the bitter winds should blow,
And all the ways be choked with snow,
'T would be a true Arabian night!

WHEN THE SULTAN GOES TO ISPAHAN.

WHEN the Sultan Shah-Zaman
Goes to the city Ispahan,
Even before he gets so far
As the place where the clustered palm-trees are,
At the last of the thirty palace-gates,
The flower of the harem, Rose-in-Bloom,
Orders a feast in his favorite room —
Glittering squares of colored ice,
Sweetened with syrop, tinctured with spice,
Creams, and cordials, and sugared dates,
Syrian apples, Othmanee quinces,
Limes, and citrons, and apricots,
And wines that are known to Eastern princes ;
And Nubian slaves, with smoking pots
Of spicéd meats and costliest fish
And all that the curious palate could wish,
Pass in and out of the cedarn doors ;
Scattered over mosaic floors
Are anemones, myrtles, and violets,
And a musical fountain throws its jets
Of a hundred colors into the air.
The dusk Sultana loosens her hair,
And stains with the henna-plant the tips
Of her pointed nails, and bites her lips

3

Till they bloom again; but, alas, *that* rose
Not for the Sultan buds and blows!
Not for the Sultan Shah-Zaman
When he goes to the city Ispahan.

Then at a wave of her sunny hand
The dancing-girls of Samarcand
Glide in like shapes from fairy-land,
Making a sudden mist in air
Of fleecy veils and floating hair
And white arms lifted. Orient blood
Runs in their veins, shines in their eyes.
And there, in this Eastern Paradise,
Filled with the breath of sandal-wood,
And Khoten musk, and aloes and myrrh,
Sits Rose-in-Bloom on a silk divan,
Sipping the wines of Astrakhan:
And her Arab lover sits with her.
That 's when the Sultan Shah-Zaman
Goes to the city Ispahan.

Now, when I see an extra light,
Flaming, flickering on the night
From my neighbor's casement opposite,
I know as well as I know to pray,
I know as well as a tongue can say,
That the innocent Sultan Shah-Zaman
Has gone to the city Ispahan.

HASCHEESH.

I.

STRICKEN with dreams, I wandered through the
    night ;
The heavens leaned down to me with splendid fires ;
The south-wind breathing upon unseen lyres
Made music as I went ; and to my sight
A Palace shaped itself against the skies :
Great sapphire-studded portals suddenly
Opened on vast Ionic galleries
Of gold and porphyry, and I could see,
Through half-drawn curtains that let in the day,
Dim tropic gardens stretching far away.

II.

Ah ! what a wonder fell upon my soul,
When from that structure of the upper airs
I saw unfold a flight of crystal stairs
For my ascending. . . . Then I heard the roll
Of unseen oceans clashing at the Pole. . . .
A terror seized upon me . . . a vague sense
Of near calamity. " O, lead me hence ! "
I shrieked, and lo ! from out a darkling hole
That opened at my feet, crawled after me,
Up the broad staircase, creatures of huge size,

Fanged, warty monsters. with their lips and eyes
Hung with slim leeches sucking hungrily. —
Away, vile drug ! I will avoid thy spell,
Honey of Paradise, black dew of Hell !

A PRELUDE.

HASSAN BEN ABDUL at the Ivory Gate
Of Bagdad sat and chattered in the sun,
Like any magpie chattered to himself
And four lank, swarthy Arab boys that stopt
A gambling game with peach-pits, and drew near.
Then Iman Khan, the friend of thirsty souls,
The seller of pure water, ceased his cry,
And placed his water-skins against the gate —
They looked so like him, with their sallow cheeks
Puffed out like Iman's. Then a eunuch came
And swung a pack of sweetmeats from his head,
And stood — a hideous pagan cut in jet.
And then a Jew. whose sandal-straps were red
With desert-dust, limped, cringing, to the crowd —
He, too, would listen ; and close after him
A jeweller that glittered like his shop.
Then two blind mendicants, who wished to go
Six diverse ways at once, came stumbling by,
But hearing Hassan chatter, sat them down.
And if the Khaleef had been riding near,
He would have paused to listen like the rest,
For Hassan's fame was ripe in all the East.
From white-walled Cairo to far Ispahan,

From Mecca to Damascus, he was known,
Hassan, the Arab with the Singing Heart.
His songs were sung by boatmen on the Nile,
By Beddowee maidens, and in Tartar camps,
While all men loved him as they loved their eyes;
And when he spake, the wisest, next to him,
Was he who listened. And thus Hassan sung.
— And I, a stranger, lingering in Bagdad,
Half English and half Arab, by my beard!
Caught at the gilded epic as it grew,
And for my Christian brothers wrote it down.

II.

INTERLUDES.

INTERLUDES.

BEFORE THE RAIN.

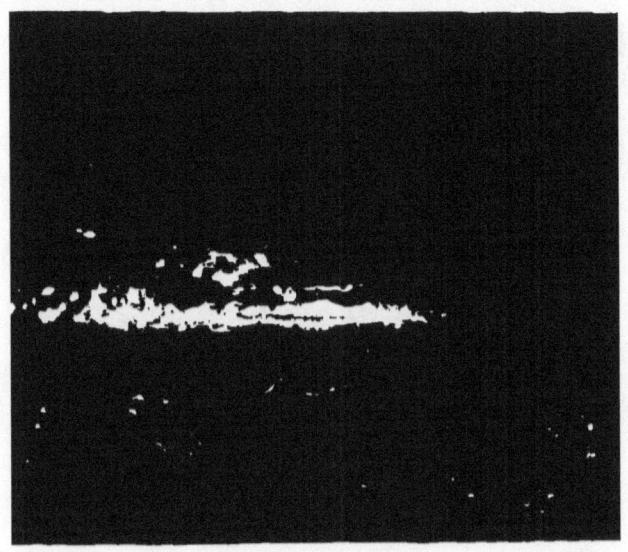

WE knew it would rain, for all the morn
  A spirit on slender ropes of mist
Was lowering its golden buckets down
  Into the vapory amethyst

Of marshes and swamps and dismal fens —
  Scooping the dew that lay in the flowers,
Dipping the jewels out of the sea,
  To sprinkle them over the land in showers.

We knew it would rain, for the poplars showed
  The white of their leaves, the amber grain
Shrunk in the wind — and the lightning now
  Is tangled in tremulous skeins of rain!

AFTER THE RAIN.

THE rain has ceased, and in my room
The sunshine pours an airy flood:
And on the church's dizzy vane
The ancient Cross is bathed in blood.

From out the dripping ivy-leaves,
Antiquely carven, gray and high,
A dormer, facing westward, looks
Upon the village like an eye:

And now it glimmers in the sun,
A square of gold, a disk, a speck:
And in the belfry sits a Dove
With purple ripples on her neck.

HESPERIDES.

If thy soul, Herrick, dwelt with me,
This is what my songs would be:
Hints of our sea-breezes, blent
With odors from the Orient;
Indian vessels deep with spice;
Star-showers from the Norland ice;
Wine-red jewels that seem to hold
Fire, but only burn with cold;
Antique goblets, strangely wrought,
Filled with the wine of happy thought;
Bridal measures, vain regrets,
Laburnum buds and violets;
Hopeful as the break of day;
Clear as crystal; new as May;
Musical as brooks that run
O'er yellow shallows in the sun;
Soft as the satin fringe that shades
The eyelids of thy fragrant maids;
Brief as thy lyrics, Herrick, are,
And polished as the bosom of a star.

CASTLES.

THERE is a picture in my brain
That only fades to come again —
The sunlight, through a veil of rain
    To leeward, gilding
A narrow stretch of brown sea-sand,
A lighthouse half a league from land,
And two young lovers, hand in hand,
    A castle-building.

Upon the budded apple-trees
The robins sing by twos and threes,
And ever, at the faintest breeze,
    Down drops a blossom;
And ever would that lover be
The wind that robs the burgeoned tree,
And lifts the soft tress daintily
    On Beauty's bosom.

Ah, graybeard, what a happy thing
It was, when life was in its spring,
To peep through love's betrothal ring
    At fields Elysian,
To move and breathe in magic air,
To think that all that seems is fair —
Ah, ripe young mouth and golden hair.
    Thou pretty vision!

Well, well, I think not on these two
But the old wound breaks out anew,
And the old dream, as if 't were true,
    In my heart nestles ;
Then tears come welling to my eyes,
For yonder, all in saintly guise,
As 't were, a sweet dead woman lies
    Upon the trestles. ·

INGRATITUDE.

FOUR bluish eggs all in the moss!
  Soft-lined home on the cherry-bough!
Life is trouble, and love is loss —
  There's only one robin now.

O robin up in the cherry-tree,
  Singing your soul away,
Great is the grief befallen me,
  And how can you be so gay?

Long ago when you cried in the nest,
  The last of the sickly brood,
Scarcely a pinfeather warming your breast,
  Who was it brought you food?

Who said, "Music, come fill his throat,
  Or ever the May be fled"?
Who was it loved the low sweet note
  And the bosom's sea-shell red?

Who said, "Cherries, grow ripe and big,
   Black and ripe for this bird of mine"?
How little bright-bosom bends the twig,
   Sipping the black-heart's wine!

Now that my days and nights are woe,
   Now that I weep for love's dear sake —
There you go singing away as though
   Never a heart could break!

DECEMBER.

ONLY the sea intoning,
Only the wainscot-mouse,
Only the wild wind moaning
Over the lonely house.

Darkest of all Decembers
Ever my life has known,
Sitting here by the embers,
Stunned and helpless, alone —

Dreaming of two graves lying
Out in the damp and chill:
One where the buzzard, flying,
Pauses at Malvern Hill:

The other — alas! the pillows
Of that uneasy bed
Rise and fall with the billows
Over our sailor's head.

DECEMBER.

Theirs the heroic story —
Died, by frigate and town!
Theirs the Calm and the Glory,
Theirs the Cross and the Crown.

Mine to linger and languish
Here by the wintry sea.
Ah, faint heart! in thy anguish,
What is there left to thee?

Only the sea intoning,
Only the wainscot-mouse,
Only the wild wind moaning
Over the lonely house.

THE FADED VIOLET.

WHAT thought is folded in thy leaves!
What tender thought, what speechless pain!
I hold thy faded lips to mine,
Thou darling of the April rain!

I hold thy faded lips to mine,
Though scent and azure tint are fled —
O dry, mute lips! ye are the type
Of something in me cold and dead:

Of something wilted like thy leaves:
Of fragrance flown, of beauty dim;
Yet, for the love of those white hands
That found thee by a river's brim —

That found thee when thy dewy mouth
Was purpled as with stains of wine —
For love of her who love forgot,
I hold thy faded lips to mine.

That thou shouldst live when I am dead,
When hate is dead, for me, and wrong,
For this, I use my subtlest art,
For this, I fold thee in my song.

AMONTILLADO.

RAFTERS black with smoke,
White with sand the floor is,
Twenty whiskered Dons
Calling to Dolores —
Tawny flower of Spain,
Wild-rose of Granada,
Keeper of the wines
In this old posada.

Hither, light-of-foot,
Dolores, Hebe, Circe! —
Pretty Spanish girl,
With not a bit of mercy!
Here I 'm sad and sick,
Faint and thirsty very,
And she does not bring
The Amontillado Sherry!

Thank you. Breath of June!
Now my heart beats free, ah!
Kisses for your hand,
Amigita mia!

4

You shall live in song,
Ripe and warm and cheery,
Mellowing with years,
Like Amontillado Sherry.

Evil spirits, fly!
Care, begone, blue dragon!
Only shapes of joy
Are sculptured on the flagon:
Lyrics — repartees —
Kisses — all that 's merry
Rise to touch the lip
In Amontillado Sherry!

Here be worth and wealth,
And love, the arch enchanter;
Here the golden blood
Of saints, in this decanter!
When old Charon comes
To row me o'er his ferry,
I 'll bribe him with a case
Of Amontillado Sherry!

While the earth spins round
And the stars lean over,
May this amber sprite
Never lack a lover.
Blessèd be the man
Who lured her from the berry,
And blest the girl who brings
The Amontillado Sherry!

What! the flagon 's dry?
Hark, old Time's confession —
Both hands crost at XII.,
Owning his transgression!
Pray, old monk! for all
Generous souls and merry,
May they have their fill
Of Amontillado Sherry!

THE LUNCH.

A GOTHIC window, where a damask curtain
Made the blank daylight shadowy and uncertain :
A slab of agate on four eagle-talons
Held trimly up and neatly taught to balance :
A porcelain dish, o'er which in many a cluster
Black grapes hung down, dead-ripe and without
       lustre :
A melon cut in thin, delicious slices :
A cake that seemed mosaic-work in spices :
Two China cups with golden tulips sunny,
And rich inside with chocolate like honey :
And she and I the banquet-scene completing
With dreamy words — and very pleasant eating !

THE ONE WHITE ROSE.

A SORROWFUL woman said to me,
"Come in and look on our child."
I saw an Angel at shut of day,
And it never spoke — but smiled.

I think of it in the city's streets,
I dream of it when I rest —
The violet eyes, the waxen hands,
And the one white rose on the breast!

NAMELESS PAIN.

In my nostrils the summer wind
Blows the exquisite scent of the rose:
O for the golden, golden wind,
Breaking the buds as it goes!
Breaking the buds and bending the grass,
And spilling the scent of the rose.

O wind of the summer morn,
Tearing the petals in twain,
Wafting the fragrant soul
Of the rose through valley and plain,
I would you could tear my heart to-day
And scatter its nameless pain!

LANDSCAPE.

TWILIGHT.

GAUNT shadows stretch along the hill;
Cold clouds drift slowly west;
Soft flocks of vagrant snow-flakes fill
The redwing's empty nest.

By sunken reefs the hoarse sea roars;
Above the shelving sands,
Like skeletons the sycamores
Uplift their wasted hands.

The air is full of hints of grief,
Strange voices touched with pain —
The pathos of the falling leaf
And rustling of the rain.

In yonder cottage shines a light,
Far-gleaming like a gem —
Not fairer to the Rabbins' sight
Was star of Bethlehem!

AT TWO-AND-TWENTY.

MARIAN, May, and Maud
  Have not past me by —
Archéd foot, and rosy mouth,
  And bronze-brown eye !

When my hair is gray,
  Then I shall be wise :
Then, thank Heaven ! I shall not care
  For bronze-brown eyes.

Then let Maud and May
  And Marian pass me by :
So they do not scorn me now,
  What care I ?

GLAMOURIE.

UNDER the night,
In the white moonshine,
Sit thou with me,
By the graveyard tree,
Imogene.

The fire-flies swarm
In the white moonshine,
Each with its light
For our bridal night,
Imogene.

Blushing with love,
In the white moonshine,
Lie in my arms,
So, safe from alarms,
Imogene.

Paler art thou
Than the white moonshine.
Ho! thou art lost —
Thou lovest a Ghost,
Imogene!

PALABRAS CARIÑOSAS.

(SPANISH AIR.)

GOOD-NIGHT! I have to say good-night
To such a host of peerless things!
Good-night unto that fragile hand
All queenly with its weight of rings;
Good-night to fond, uplifted eyes,
Good-night to chestnut braids of hair,
Good-night unto the perfect mouth,
And all the sweetness nestled there —
   The snowy hand detains me, then
   I 'll have to say Good-night again!

But there will come a time, my love,
When, if I read our stars aright,
I shall not linger by this porch
With my adieus. Till then, good-night!
You wish the time were now? And I.
You do not blush to wish it so?
You would have blushed yourself to death
To own so much a year ago —
   What, both these snowy hands! ah, then
   I 'll have to say Good-night again!

MAY.

HEBE 's here, May is here!
The air is fresh and sunny;
And the miser-bees are busy
Hoarding golden honey.

See the knots of buttercups,
And the purple pansies —
Thick as these, within my brain,
Grow the .wildest fancies.

Let me write my songs to-day.
Rhymes with dulcet closes —
Four-line epics one might hide
In the hearts of roses.

THE BLUEBELLS OF NEW ENGLAND.

THE roses are a regal troop,
And modest folk the daisies:
But, Bluebells of New England,
To you I give my praises —

To you, fair phantoms in the sun,
Whom merry Spring discovers,
With bluebirds for your laureates,
And honey-bees for lovers.

The south-wind breathes, and lo! you throng
This rugged land of ours:
I think the pale blue clouds of May
Drop down, and turn to flowers!

By cottage doors along the roads
You show your winsome faces,
And, like the spectre lady, haunt
The lonely woodland places.

All night your eyes are closed in sleep,
Kept fresh for day's adorning:
Such simple faith as yours can see
God's coming in the morning!

You lead me by your holiness
To pleasant ways of duty;
You set my thoughts to melody,
You fill me with your beauty.

Long may the heavens give you rain,
The sunshine its caresses,
Long may the woman that I love
Entwine you in her tresses!

WEDDED.

(PROVENÇAL AIR.)

THE happy bells shall ring,
    Marguerite;
The summer birds shall sing,
    Marguerite —
You smile, but you shall wear
Orange-blossoms in your hair,
    Marguerite.

Ah me! the bells have rung,
    Marguerite;
The summer birds have sung,
    Marguerite —
But cypress leaf and rue
Make a sorry wreath for you,
    Marguerite.

ROMANCE.

I.

I HAVE placed a golden
Ring upon the hand
Of the blithest little
Lady in the land!

When the early roses
Scent the sunny air,
She shall gather white ones
To tremble in her hair!

Hasten, happy roses,
Come to me by May —
In your folded petals
Lies my wedding-day.

II.

The chestnuts shine through the cloven rind,
  And the woodland leaves are red, my dear:
The scarlet fuchsias burn in the wind —
  Funeral plumes for the Year!

The Year which has brought me so much woe
  That if it were not for you, my dear,

I could wish the fuchsias' fire might glow
For me as well as the Year.

III.

Out from the depths of my heart
Had arisen this single cry,
Let me behold my belovéd,
Let me behold her, and die.

At last, like a sinful soul
At the portals of Heaven I lie,
Never to walk with the blest,
Ah, never! . . . only to die.

DESTINY.

THREE roses, wan as moonlight and weighed down
Each with its loveliness as with a crown,
Drooped in a florist's window in a town.

The first a lover bought. It lay at rest,
Like flower on flower, that night, on Beauty's breast.

The second rose, as virginal and fair,
Shrunk in the tangles of a harlot's hair.

The third, a widow, with new grief made wild,
Shut in the icy palm of her dead child.

UNSUNG.

As sweet as the breath that goes
From the lips of the white rose,
As weird as the elfin lights
That glimmer of frosty nights,
As wild as the winds that tear
The curled red leaf in the air,
Is the song I have never sung.

In slumber, a hundred times
I have said the mystic rhymes,
But ere I open my eyes
This ghost of a poem flies;
Of the interfluent strains
Not even a note remains:
I know by my pulses' beat
It was something wild and sweet,
And my heart is strangely stirred
By an unremembered word!

I strive, but I strive in vain,
To recall the lost refrain.
On some miraculous day
Perhaps it will come and stay;
In some unimagined Spring
I may find my voice, and sing
The song I have never sung.

FROST-WORK.

THESE winter nights, against my window-pane
Nature with busy pencil draws designs
Of ferns and blossoms and fine spray of pines,
Oak-leaf and acorn and fantastic vines,
Which she will make when summer comes again —
Quaint arabesques in argent, flat and cold,
Like curious Chinese etchings. . . . By and by,
Walking my leafy garden as of old,
These frosty fantasies shall charm my eye
In azure, damask, emerald, and gold.

ROCOCO.

By studying my lady's eyes
I've grown so learnéd day by day,
So Machiavelian in this wise,
That when I send her flowers, I say

To each small flower (no matter what,
Geranium, pink, or tuberose,
Syringa, or forget-me-not,
Or violet) before it goes:

" Be not triumphant, little flower,
When on her haughty heart you lie,
But modestly enjoy your hour:
She'll weary of you by and by."

HAUNTED.

A NOISOME mildewed vine
Crawls to the rotting eaves;
The gate has dropped from the rusty hinge,
And the walks are stamped with leaves.

Close by the shattered fence
The red-clay road runs by
To a haunted wood, where the hemlocks groan
And the willows sob and sigh.

Among the dank lush flowers
The spiteful fire-fly glows,
And a woman steals by the stagnant pond
Wrapt in her burial clothes.

There's a dark blue scar on her throat,
And ever she makes a moan,
And the humid lizards gleam in the grass,
And the lichens weep on the stone;

And the Moon shrinks in a cloud,
And the traveller shakes with fear,
And an Owl on the skirts of the wood
Hoots, and says, Do you hear?

Go not there at night,
For a spell hangs over all —
The palsied elms, and the dismal road,
And the broken garden-wall.

O. go not there at night,
For a curse is on the place;
Go not there, for fear you meet
The Murdered face to face!

FABLE.

ROME, 1875.

A CERTAIN bird in a certain wood,
Feeling the spring-time warm and good,
Sang to it, in melodious mood.
On other neighboring branches stood
Other birds who heard his song:
Loudly he sang, and clear and strong;
Sweetly he sang, and it stirred their gall
There should be a voice so musical.
They said to themselves : "We must stop that
        bird,
He 's the sweetest voice was ever heard.
That rich, deep chest-note, crystal-clear,
Is a mortifying thing to hear.
We have sharper beaks and hardier wings,
Yet we but croak: *this* fellow sings!"

So they planned and planned, and killed the bird
With the sweetest voice was ever heard.

Passing his grave one happy May,
I brought this English daisy away.

A SNOW-FLAKE.

ONCE he sang of summer,
Nothing but the summer ;
Now he sings of winter,
Of winter bleak and drear :
Just because there 's fallen
A snow-flake on his forehead,
He must go and fancy
'T is winter all the year !

IDENTITY.

SOMEWHERE — in desolate wind-swept space —
In Twilight-land — in No-man's-land —
Two hurrying Shapes met face to face,
And bade each other stand.

" And who are you ? " cried one, agape,
Shuddering in the gloaming light.
" I know not," said the second Shape,
" I only died last night ! "

ACROSS THE STREET.

WITH lash on cheek, she comes and goes;
I watch her when she little knows :
   I wonder if she dreams of it.
Sitting and working at my rhymes,
I weave into my verse at times
   Her sunny hair, or gleams of it.

Upon her window-ledge is set
A box of flowering mignonette;
   Morning and eve she tends to them —
The senseless flowers, that do not care
About that loosened strand of hair,
   As prettily she bends to them.

If I could once contrive to get
Into that box of mignonette
   Some morning when she tends to them —
She comes! I see the rich blood rise
From throat to cheek! — down go the eyes.
   Demurely, as she bends to them !

NOCTURNE.

BELLAGGIO.

Up to her chamber window
A slight wire trellis goes,
And up this Romeo's ladder
Clambers a bold white rose.

I lounge in the ilex shadows,
I see the lady lean,
Unclasping her silken girdle,
The curtain's folds between.

She smiles on her white-rose lover,
She reaches out her hand
And helps him in at the window —
I see it where I stand!

To her scarlet lip she holds him,
And kisses him many a time —
Ah, me! it was he that won her
Because he dared to climb!

AN UNTIMELY THOUGHT.

I WONDER what day of the week —
I wonder what month of the year —
Will it be midnight, or morning,
And who will bend over my bier?

— What a hideous fancy to come
As I wait, at the foot of the stair,
While Lilian gives the last touch
To her robe, or the rose in her hair.

Do I like your new dress — pompadour?
And do I like *you?* On my life,
You are eighteen, and not a day more,
And have not been six years my wife.

Those two rosy boys in the crib
Up-stairs are not ours, to be sure! —
You are just a sweet bride in her bloom,
All sunshine, and snowy, and pure.

As the carriage rolls down the dark street
The little wife laughs and makes cheer —
But . . . I wonder what day of the week,
I wonder what month of the year.

RENCONTRE.

TOILING across the Mer de Glace,
I thought of, longed for thee;
What miles between us stretched, alas! —
What miles of land and sea!

My foe, undreamed of, at my side
Stood suddenly, like Fate.
For those who love, the world is wide,
But not for those who hate.

LOVE'S CALENDAR.

THE Summer comes and the Summer goes;
   Wild-flowers are fringing the dusty lanes,
   The swallows go darting through fragrant rains,
Then, all of a sudden — it snows.

Dear Heart, our lives so happily flow,
   So lightly we heed the flying hours,
   We only know Winter is gone — by the flowers,
We only know Winter is come — by the snow.

A WINTER-PIECE.

Sous le voile qui vous protége,
Défiant les regards jaloux,
Si vous sortez par cette neige,
Redoutez vos pieds andalous.

TnÉOPHILE GAUTIER.

BENEATH the heavy veil you wear,
Shielded from jealous eyes you go:
But of your pretty feet have care
If you should venture through the snow.

Howe'er you tread, a dainty mould
Betrays that light foot all the same;
Upon this glistening, snowy fold
At every step it signs your name.

Thus guided, one might come too close
Upon the slyly-hidden nest
Where Psyche, with her cheek's cold rose,
On Love's warm bosom lies at rest.

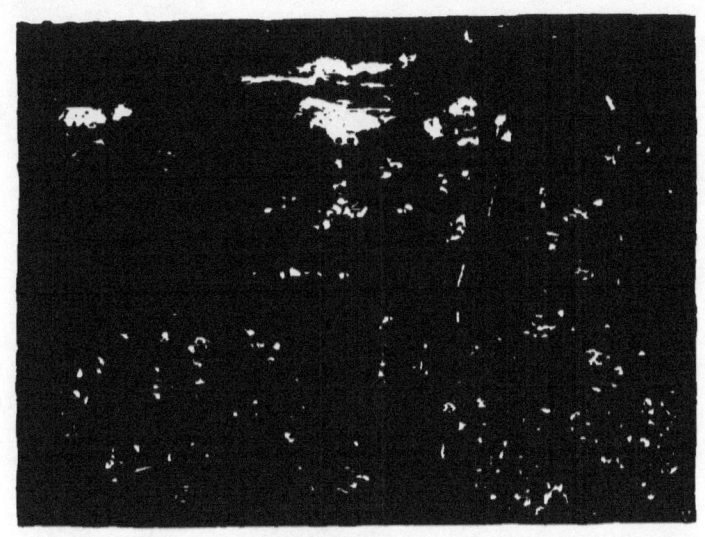

QUATRAINS.

1.

DAY AND NIGHT.

DAY is a snow-white Dove of heaven
That from the East glad message brings:
Night is a stealthy, evil Raven,
Wrapped to the eyes in his black wings.

2.

MAPLE LEAVES.

OCTOBER turned my maple's leaves to gold;
The most are gone now; here and there one lingers:
Soon these will slip from out the twigs' weak hold,
Like coins between a dying miser's fingers.

3.

A CHILD'S GRAVE.

A LITTLE mound with chipped headstone,
The grass, ah me! uncut about the sward.
    Summer by summer left alone
With one white lily keeping watch and ward.

4.

PESSIMIST AND OPTIMIST.

THIS one sits shivering in Fortune's smile,
Taking his joy with bated, doubtful breath:
This other, gnawed by hunger, all the while
    Laughs in the teeth of Death.

5.

GRACE AND STRENGTH.

MANOAH's son, in his blind rage malign
Tumbling the temple down upon his foes,
Did no such feat as yonder delicate vine
That day by day untired holds up a rose.

6.

AMONG THE PINES.

FAINT murmurs from the pine-tops reach my ear,
As if a harp-string — touched in some far sphere —
Vibrating in the lucid atmosphere,
Let the soft south wind waft its music here.

7.

FROM THE SPANISH.

To him that hath, we are told,
Shall be given. Yes, by the Cross!
To the rich man fate sends gold,
To the poor man loss on loss.

8.

MASKS.

BLACK Tragedy lets slip her grim disguise
And shows you laughing lips and roguish eyes;
But when, unmasked, gay Comedy appears,
'T is ten to one you find the girl in tears.

9.

COQUETTE.

OR light or dark, or short or tall,
She sets a springe to snare them all;
All 's one to her — above her fan
She 'd make sweet eyes at Caliban.

10.

EPITAPHS.

Honest Iago. When his breath was fled
Doubtless these words were carven at his head.
Such lying epitaphs are like a rose
That in unlovely earth takes root and grows.

11.

POPULARITY.

Such kings of shreds have wooed and won her,
  Such crafty knaves her laurel owned,
It has become almost an honor
    Not to be crowned.

12.

HUMAN IGNORANCE.

What mortal knows
Whence come the tint and odor of the rose?
  What probing deep
Has ever solved the mystery of sleep?

13.

SPENDTHRIFT.

The fault 's not mine, you understand:
  God shaped my palm so I can hold
But little water in my hand
    And not much gold.

14.

THE IRON AGE.

The wide-lipped Sphinx, with bent perplexéd brow,
Crouches in desert sand, inert and pale,
Hearing the engine's raucous scream, that now
Sends Echo flying through the Memphian vale.

15.

ON READING ——.

GREAT thoughts in crude, inadequate verse set forth,
Lose half their preciousness, and ever must.
Unless the diamond with its own rich dust
Be cut and polished, it seems little worth.

16.

THE ROSE.

FIXED to her necklace, like another gem,
A rose she wore — the flower June made for her;
Fairer it looked than when upon the stem,
And must, indeed, have been much happier.

17.

MOONRISE AT SEA.

UP from the dark the moon begins to creep;
And now a pallid, haggard face lifts she
Above the water-line: thus from the deep
A drownéd body rises solemnly.

18.

THE DIFFERENCE.

SOME weep because they part,
And languish broken-hearted,
And others — O my heart! —
Because they never parted.

19.

FROM EASTERN SOURCES.

I.

In youth my hair was black as night,
My life as white as driven snow:
As white as snow my hair is now,
And that is black which once was white.

II.

No wonder Sajib wrote such verses, when
He had the bill of nightingale for pen;
Or that his lyrics were divine
Whose only ink was tears and wine.

III.

A poor dwarf's figure, looming through the dense
Mists of a mountain, seemed a shape immense,
On seeing which, a giant, in dismay,
　　Took to his heels and ran away.

20.

THE PARCÆ.

In their dark House of Cloud
The three weird sisters toil till time be sped:
One unwinds life; one ever weaves the shroud;
　　One waits to cut the thread.

PALINODE.

I.

WHEN I was young and light of heart
I made sad songs with easy art:
Now I am sad, and no more young,
My sorrow cannot find a tongue.

II.

Pray, Muses, since I may not sing
Of Death or any grievous thing,
Teach me some joyous strain, that I
May mock my youth's hypocrisy!

III.

SPRING IN NEW ENGLAND

AND OTHER POEMS.

SPRING IN NEW ENGLAND

AND OTHER POEMS.

SPRING IN NEW ENGLAND.

I.

THE long years come and go,
   And the Past,
The sorrowful, splendid Past,
With its glory and its woe,
   Seems never to have been.
The bugle's taunting blast
Has died away by Southern ford and glen:
The mock-bird sings unfrightened in its dell;
The ensanguined stream flows pure again;
Where once the hissing death-bolt fell,
And all along the artillery's level lines
   Leapt flames of hell,
The farmer smiles upon the sprouting grain,
   And tends his vines.
Seems never to have been?
  O sombre days and grand,
   How ye crowd back once more,
Seeing our heroes' graves are green
  By the Potomac and the Cumberland,
   And in the valley of the Shenandoah!

II.

Now while the pale arbutus in our woods
Wakes to faint life beneath the dead year's leaves,
And the bleak North lets loose its wailing broods
Of winds upon us, and the gray sea grieves
Along our coast; while yet the Winter's hand
Heavily presses on New England's heart,
And Spring averts the sunshine of her eyes
Lest some vain cowslip should untimely start —
While we are housed in this rude season's gloom,
　　In this rude land,
　　Bereft of warmth and bloom,
We know, far off beneath the Southern skies,
Where the flush blossoms mock our drifts of snow
And the lithe vine unfolds its emerald sheen —
On many a sunny hillside there, we know
　　Our heroes' graves are green.

III.

　　The long years come, but *they*
　　　　Come not again!
　　Through vapors dense and gray
　　　　Steals back the May,
　　But they come not again —
　　　　Swept by the battle's fiery breath
　　　　Down unknown ways of death.
　　How can our fancies help but go
　　Out from this realm of mist and rain,
　　Out from this realm of sleet and snow,
　　When the first Southern violets blow?

IV.

While yet the year is young
Many a garland shall be hung
  In our gardens of the dead;
On obelisk and urn
Shall the lilac's purple burn,
  And the wild-rose leaves be shed.
And afar in the woodland ways,
Through the rustic church-yard gate
Matrons and maidens shall pass,
Striplings and white-haired men,
And, spreading aside the grass,
Linger at name and date,
Remembering old, old days!
And the lettering on each stone
Where the mould's green breath has blown
Tears shall wash clear again !.

V.

But far away to the South, in the sultry, stricken
    land —
On the banks of silvery streams gurgling among their
    reeds,
By many a drear morass, where the long-necked peli-
    can feeds,
By many a dark bayou, and blinding dune of sand,
By many a cypress swamp where the cayman seeks
    its prey,
In many a moss-hung wood, the twilight's haunt by
    day,

And down where the land's parched lip drinks at the
    salt sea-waves,
And the ghostly sails glide by — there are piteous
    nameless graves.

Their names no tongue may tell,
Buried there where they fell,
The bravest of our braves!
Never sweetheart, or friend,
    Wan pale mother, or bride,

Over these mounds shall bend,
  Tenderly putting aside
The unremembering grass!
  Never the votive wreath
  For the unknown brows beneath,
Never a tear, alas!
How can our fancies help but go
Out from this realm of mist and rain,
Out from this realm of sleet and snow,
When the first Southern violets blow?
How must our thought bend over them,
Blessing the flowers that cover them —
  Piteous, nameless graves!

VI.

Ah. but the life they gave
Is not shut in the grave:
The valorous spirits freed
Live in the vital deed!
Marble shall crumble to dust,
Plinth of bronze and of stone,
Carved escutcheon and crest —
Silently, one by one,
The sculptured lilies fall:
Softly the tooth of the rust
Gnaws through the brazen shield:
Broken, and covered with stains,
The crossed stone swords must yield:
Mined by the frost and the drouth,
Smitten by north and south,
Smitten by east and west,
Down comes column and all!
But the great deed remains.

VII.

When we remember how they died —
In dark ravine and on the mountain-side,
In leaguered fort and fire-encircled town,
Upon the gun-boat's splintered deck,
And where the iron ships went down —
How their dear lives were spent,
In the crushed and reddened wreck,
By lone lagoons and streams,
In the weary hospital-tent,
In the cockpit's crowded hive —
How they languished and died
In the black stockades — it seems
Ignoble to be alive!
Tears will well to our eyes,
And the bitter doubt will rise —
But hush! for the strife is done,
Forgiven are wound and scar:
The fight was fought and won
Long since, on sea and shore,
And every scattered star
Set in the blue once more:
We are one as before,
With the blot from our scutcheon gone!

VIII.

So let our heroes rest
Upon your sunny breast:
Keep them, O South, our tender hearts and true,
Keep them, O South, and learn to hold them dear
From year to year!

Never forget,
Dying for us, they died for you.
This hallowed dust should knit us closer yet.

IX.

Hark ! 't is the bluebird's venturous strain
  High on the old fringed elm at the gate —
      Sweet-voiced, valiant on the swaying bough,
        Alert, elate,
    Dodging the fitful spits of snow,
New England's poet-laureate
Telling us Spring has come again !

7

BABY BELL.

I.

HAVE you not heard the poets tell
  How came the dainty Baby Bell
  Into this world of ours?
The gates of heaven were left ajar:
With folded hands and dreamy eyes,
Wandering out of Paradise,
She saw this planet, like a star,
  Hung in the glistening depths of even —
Its bridges, running to and fro,
O'er which the white-winged Angels go,
  Bearing the holy Dead to heaven.
She touched a bridge of flowers — those feet,
So light they did not bend the bells
Of the celestial asphodels,

They fell like dew upon the flowers:
Then all the air grew strangely sweet!
And thus came dainty Baby Bell
  Into this world of ours.

II.

She came and brought delicious May.
  The swallows built beneath the eaves;
  Like sunlight, in and out the leaves
The robins went, the livelong day;
The lily swung its noiseless bell;
  And o'er the porch the trembling vine
  Seemed bursting with its veins of wine.
How sweetly, softly, twilight fell!
O, earth was full of singing-birds
And opening springtide flowers,
When the dainty Baby Bell
  Came to this world of ours!

III.

  O Baby, dainty Baby Bell,
How fair she grew from day to day!
  What woman-nature filled her eyes,
What poetry within them lay —
Those deep and tender twilight eyes,
  So full of meaning, pure and bright
  As if she yet stood in the light
Of those oped gates of Paradise.
And so we loved her more and more:
  Ah, never in our hearts before
  Was love so lovely born!
We felt we had a link between

This real world and that unseen —
    The land beyond the morn;
And for the love of those dear eyes,
For love of her whom God led forth,
(The mother's being ceased on earth
When Baby came from Paradise,) —
For love of Him who smote our lives,
    And woke the chords of joy and pain,
We said, *Dear Christ!* — our hearts bent down
    Like violets after rain.

IV.

And now the orchards, which were white
    And red with blossoms when she came,
Were rich in autumn's mellow prime:
The clustered apples burnt like flame,
The soft-cheeked peaches blushed and fell,
The folded chestnut burst its shell,
The grapes hung purpling in the grange:
And time wrought just as rich a change
    In little Baby Bell.
Her lissome form more perfect grew,
    And in her features we could trace,
    In softened curves, her mother's face.
Her angel-nature ripened too:
We thought her lovely when she came,
    But she was holy, saintly now . . .
    Around her pale angelic brow
We saw a slender ring of flame!

v.

God's hand had taken away the seal
  That held the portals of her speech;
And oft she said a few strange words
  Whose meaning lay beyond our reach.
She never was a child to us,
We never held her being's key;
We could not teach her holy things:
She was Christ's self in purity.

vi.

It came upon us by degrees,
We saw its shadow ere it fell —
The knowledge that our God had sent
His messenger for Baby Bell.
We shuddered with unlanguaged pain,
And all our hopes were changed to fears,
And all our thoughts ran into tears
Like sunshine into rain.
We cried aloud in our belief,
"O, smite us gently, gently, God!
Teach us to bend and kiss the rod,
And perfect grow through grief."
Ah! how we loved her, God can tell;
Her heart was folded deep in ours.
Our hearts are broken, Baby Bell!

vii.

At last he came, the messenger,
  The messenger from unseen lands:
And what did dainty Baby Bell?

She only crossed her little hands,
She only looked more meek and fair!
We parted back her silken hair,
We wove the roses round her brow —
White buds, the summer's drifted snow, —
Wrapt her from head to foot in flowers . . .
And thus went dainty Baby Bell
   Out of this world of ours!

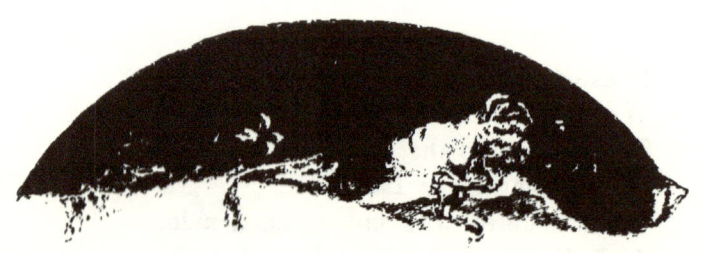

PAMPINA.

LYING by the summer sea
I had a dream of Italy.

Chalky cliffs and miles of sand,
Mossy reefs and salty caves,
Then the sparkling emerald waves,
Faded; and I seemed to stand,
Myself a languid Florentine,
In the heart of that fair land.
And in a garden cool and green,
Boccaccio's own enchanted place,
I met Pampina face to face —
A maid so lovely that to see
Her smile is to know Italy!
Her hair was like a coronet
Upon her Grecian forehead set,
Where one gem glistened sunnily
Like Venice, when first seen at sea.
I saw within her violet eyes
The starlight of Italian skies,
And on her brow and breast and hand
The olive of her native land!

And, knowing how in other times
Her lips were ripe with Tuscan rhymes

Of love and wine and dance, I spread
My mantle by an almond-tree,
And " Here, beneath the rose," I said,
" I 'll hear thy Tuscan melody."
I heard a tale that was not told
In those ten dreamy days of old,
When Heaven, for some divine offence,
Smote Florence with the pestilence ;
And in that garden's odorous shade
The dames of the Decameron,
With each a loyal lover, strayed,
To laugh and sing, at sorest need,
To lie in the lilies in the sun
With glint of plume and silver brede.
And while she whispers in my ear,
The pleasant Arno murmurs near,
The dewy, slim chameleons run
Through twenty colors in the sun ;
The breezes blur the fountain's glass,
And wake Æolian melodies,
And scatter from the scented trees
The lemon-blossoms on the grass.

The tale ? I have forgot the tale —
A Lady all for love forlorn,
A rosebud, and a nightingale
That bruised his bosom on the thorn ;
A jar of rubies buried deep,
A glen, a corpse, a child asleep,
A Monk, that was no monk at all,
In the moonlight by a castle-wall.

Now while the large-eyed Tuscan wove
The gilded thread of her romance —
Which I have lost by grievous chance —
The one dear woman that I love,
Beside me in our seaside nook,
Closed a white finger in her book,
Half vext that she should read, and weep
For Petrarch, to a man asleep!
And scorning me, so tame and cold,
She rose, and wandered down the shore,
Her wine-dark drapery, fold in fold,
Imprisoned by an ivory hand;
And on a bowlder, half in sand,
She stood, and looked at Appledore.

And waking, I beheld her there
Sea-dreaming in the moted air,
A siren lithe and debonair,
With wristlets woven of scarlet weeds,
And oblong lucent amber beads
Of sea-kelp shining in her hair.
And as I thought of dreams, and how
The something in us never sleeps,
But laughs, or sings, or moans, or weeps,
She turned — and on her breast and brow
I saw the tint that seemed not won
From kisses of New England sun;
I saw on brow and breast and hand
The olive of a sunnier land!
She turned — and, lo! within her eyes
There lay the starlight of Italian skies.

Most dreams are dark, beyond the range
Of reason ; oft we cannot tell
If they are born of heaven or hell;
But to my soul it seems not strange
That, lying by the summer sea,
With that dark woman watching me,
I slept and dreamed of Italy!

LAMIA.

Go on your way, and let me pass.
You stop a wild despair.
I would that I were turned to brass
Like that chained lion there,

Which, couchant by the postern gate,
In weather foul or fair,
Looks down serenely desolate,
And nothing does but stare!

Ah, what 's to me the burgeoned year,
The sad leaf or the gay?
Let Launcelot and Queen Guinevere
Their falcons fly this day.

'T will be as royal sport, pardie,
As falconers have tried
At Astolat — but let me be !
I would that I had died.

I met a woman in the glade:
Her hair was soft and brown,
And long bent silken lashes weighed
Her ivory eyelids down.

I kissed her hand, I called her blest,
I held her leal and fair —
She turned to shadow on my breast,
And melted into air!

And, lo! about me, fold on fold,
A writhing serpent hung —
An eye of jet, a skin of gold,
A garnet for a tongue!

O, let the petted falcons fly
Right merry in the sun ;
But let me be! for I shall die
Before the year is done.

INVOCATION TO SLEEP.

I.

THERE is a rest for all things. On still nights
   There is a folding of a million wings —
The swarming honey-bees in unknown woods,
The speckled butterflies, and downy broods
       In dizzy poplar heights :
Rest for innumerable nameless things.
Rest for the creatures underneath the Sea,
   And in the Earth, and in the starry Air . . .
   Why will it not unburden me of care ?
   It comes to meaner things than my despair.
O weary, weary night, that brings no rest to me !

II.

Spirit of dreams and silvern memories,
       Delicate Sleep !
One who is sickening of his tiresome days
Brings thee a soul that he would have thee keep
A captive in thy mystical domain,
With Puck and Ariel, and the grotesque train
That people slumber. Give his sight
Immortal shapes, and bring to him again
His Psyche that went out into the night !

III.

Thou who dost hold the priceless keys of rest,
Strew lotus-leaves and poppies on my breast,
   And bear me to thy castle in the land
Touched with all colors like a burning west —
The Castle of Vision, where the unchecked thought
Wanders at will upon enchanted ground,
       Making no sound
       In all the corridors . . .
The bell sleeps in the belfry — from its tongue
A drowsy murmur floats into the air,
Like thistle-down. Slumber is everywhere.
The rook 's asleep, and, in its dreaming, caws ;
And silence mopes where nightingales have sung ;
The Sirens lie in grottos cool and deep,
   The Naiads in the streams :
But I, in chilling twilight, stand and wait
At the portcullis, at thy castle gate,
Yearning to see the magic door of dreams
Turn on its noiseless hinges, delicate Sleep !

SEADRIFT.

See where she stands, on the wet sea-sands,
   Looking across the water:
Wild is the night, but wilder still
   The face of the fisher's daughter!

What does she there, in the lightning's glare,
   What does she there, I wonder?
What dread demon drags her forth
   In the night and wind and thunder?

Is it the ghost that haunts this coast? —
   The cruel waves mount higher,
And the beacon pierces the stormy dark
   With its javelin of fire.

Beyond the light of the beacon bright
   A merchantman is tacking;
The hoarse wind whistling through the shrouds,
   And the brittle topmasts cracking.

The sea it moans over dead men's bones,
   The sea it foams in anger;
The curlews swoop through the resonant air
   With a warning cry of danger.

The star-fish clings to the sea-weed's rings
 In a vague, dumb sense of peril;
And the spray, with its phantom-fingers, grasps
 At the mullein dry and sterile.

O, who is she that stands by the sea,
 In the lightning's glare, undaunted? —
Seems this now like the coast of hell
 By one white spirit haunted!

The night drags by; and the breakers die
 Along the ragged ledges;
The robin stirs in its drenchéd nest,
 The hawthorn blooms on the hedges.

In shimmering lines, through the dripping pines,
 The stealthy morn advances;
And the heavy sea-fog straggles back
 Before those bristling lances!

Still she stands on the wet sea-sands;
 The morning breaks above her,
And the corpse of a sailor gleams on the rocks —
 What if it were her lover?

8

IN THE OLD CHURCH TOWER.

In the old church tower
    Hangs the bell;
And above it on the vane,
In the sunshine and the rain,
Cut in gold, St. Peter stands,
With the keys in his claspt hands,
    And all is well.

In the old church tower
    Hangs the bell:
You can hear its great heart beat,
Ah! so loud, and wild, and sweet,
As the parson says a prayer
Over wedded lovers there,
    And all is well.

In the old church tower
    Hangs the bell;
Deep and solemn, hark! again,
Ah, what passion and what pain!
With her hands upon her breast,
Some poor Soul has gone to rest
    Where all is well.

In the old church tower
    Hangs the bell —
An old friend that seems to know
All our joy and all our woe;
It is glad when we are wed,
It is sad when we are dead,
    And all is well!

PISCATAQUA RIVER.

THOU singest by the gleaming isles,
By woods, and fields of corn,
Thou singest, and the sunlight smiles
Upon my birthday morn.

But I within a city, I,
So full of vague unrest,
Would almost give my life to lie
An hour upon thy breast!

To let the wherry listless go,
And, wrapt in dreamy joy,
Dip, and surge idly to and fro,
Like the red harbor-buoy;

To sit in happy indolence,
To rest upon the oars,
And catch the heavy earthy scents
That blow from summer shores;

To see the rounded sun go down,
And with its parting fires
Light up the windows of the town
And burn the tapering spires:

And then to hear the muffled tolls
From steeples slim and white,
And watch, among the Isles of Shoals,
The Beacon's orange light.

O River! flowing to the main
Through woods, and fields of corn,
Hear thou my longing and my pain
This sunny birthday morn:

And take this song which sorrow shapes
To music like thine own,
And sing it to the cliffs and capes
And crags where I am known!

THE FLIGHT OF THE GODDESS.

A MAN should live in a garret aloof,
And have few friends, and go poorly clad,
With an old hat stopping the chink in the roof,
To keep the Goddess constant and glad.

Of old, when I walked on a rugged way,
And gave much work for but little bread,
The Goddess dwelt with me night and day,
Sat at my table, haunted my bed.

The narrow, mean attic, I see it now! —
Its window o'erlooking the city's tiles,
The sunset's fires, and the clouds of snow,
And the river wandering miles and miles.

Just one picture hung in the room,
The saddest story that Art can tell —
Dante and Virgil in lurid gloom
Watching the Lovers float through Hell.

Wretched enough was I sometimes,
Pinched, and harassed with vain desires;
But thicker than clover sprung the rhymes
As I dwelt like a sparrow among the spires.

Midnight filled my slumbers with song ;
Music haunted my dreams by day ·
Now I listen and wait and long,
But the Delphian airs have died away.

I wonder and wonder how it befell :
Suddenly I had friends in crowds ;
I bade the house-tops a long farewell ;
" Good-by," I cried, " to the stars and clouds !

" But thou, rare soul, that hast dwelt with me,
Spirit of Poesy ! thou divine
Breath of the morning, thou shalt be,
Goddess ! for ever and ever mine."

And the woman I loved was now my bride,
And the house I wanted was my own ;
I turned to the Goddess satisfied —
But the Goddess had somehow flown !

Flown, and I fear she will never return ;
I am much too sleek and happy for her,
Whose lovers must hunger, and waste, and burn,
Ere the beautiful heathen heart will stir !

I call — but she does not stoop to my cry ;
I wait — but she lingers, and ah ! so long !
It was not so in the years gone by,
When she touched my lips with chrism of song.

I swear I will get me a garret again,
And adore, like a Parsee, the sunset's fires,

And lure the Goddess, by vigil and pain,
Up with the sparrows among the spires.

For a man should live in a garret aloof,
And have few friends, and go poorly clad,
With an old hat stopping the chink in the roof,
To keep the Goddess constant and glad.

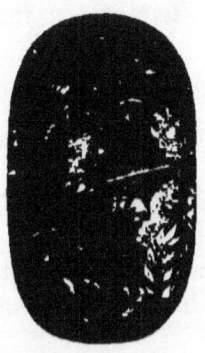

ON AN INTAGLIO HEAD OF MINERVA.

BENEATH the warrior's helm, behold
  The flowing tresses of the woman!
Minerva, Pallas, what you will —
  A winsome creature, Greek or Roman.

Minerva? No! 't is some sly minx
  In cousin's helmet masquerading;
If not — then Wisdom was a dame
  For sonnets and for serenading!

I thought the goddess cold, austere,
  Not made for love's despairs and blisses:

Did Pallas wear her hair like that?
  Was Wisdom's mouth so shaped for kisses?

The Nightingale should be her bird,
  And not the Owl, big-eyed and solemn:
How very fresh she looks, and yet
  She 's older far than Trajan's Column!

The magic hand that carved this face,
  And set this vine-work round it running,
Perhaps ere mighty Phidias wrought
  Had lost its subtle skill and cunning.

Who was he? Was he glad or sad,
  Who knew to carve in such a fashion?
Perchance he graved the dainty head
  For some brown girl that scorned his passion.

Perchance, in some still garden-place,
  Where neither fount nor tree to-day is,
He flung the jewel at the feet
  Of Phryne, or perhaps 't was Laïs.

But he is dust; we may not know
  His happy or unhappy story:
Nameless, and dead these centuries,
  His work outlives him — there 's his glory!

Both man and jewel lay in earth
  Beneath a lava-buried city;
The countless summers came and went
  With neither haste, nor hate, nor pity.

Years blotted out the man, but left
 The jewel fresh as any blossom,
Till some Visconti dug it up —
 To rise and fall on Mabel's bosom!

O nameless brother! see how Time
 Your gracious handiwork has guarded:
See how your loving, patient art
 Has come, at last, to be rewarded.

Who would not suffer slights of men,
 And pangs of hopeless passion also,
To have his carven agate-stone
 On such a bosom rise and fall so!

AN OLD CASTLE.

I.

THE gray arch crumbles,
And totters, and tumbles ;
The bat has built in the banquet hall;
In the donjon-keep
Sly mosses creep ;
The ivy has scaled the southern wall :
No man-at-arms
Sounds quick alarms
A-top of the cracked martello tower :
The drawbridge-chain
Is broken in twain —
The bridge will neither rise nor lower.

Not any manner
Of broidered banner
Flaunts at a blazoned herald's call.
Lilies float
In the stagnant moat ;
And fair they are, and tall.

II.

Here, in the old
Forgotten springs,
Was wassail held by queens and kings ;
Here at the board
Sat clown and lord,
Maiden fair and lover bold,
Baron fat and minstrel lean,
The prince with his stars,
The knight with his scars,
The priest in his gabardine.

III.

Where is she
Of the fleur-de-lys,
And that true knight who wore her gages ?
Where are the glances
That bred wild fancies
In curly heads of my lady's pages ?
Where are those
Who, in steel or hose,
Held revel here, and made them gay ?
Where is the laughter
That shook the rafter —
Where is the rafter, by the way ?

Gone is the roof,
And perched aloof
Is an owl, like a friar of Orders Gray.
(Perhaps 't is the priest
Come back to feast —
He had ever a tooth for capon, he!
But the capon's cold,
And the steward's old,
And the butler's lost the larder-key!)
The doughty lords
Sleep the sleep of swords.
Dead are the dames and damozels.
The King in his crown
Hath laid him down,
And the Jester with his bells.

IV.

All is dead here:
Poppies are red here,
Vines in my lady's chamber grow —
If 't was her chamber
Where they clamber
Up from the poisonous weeds below.
All is dead here,
Joy is fled here;
Let us hence. 'T is the end of all —
The gray arch crumbles,
And totters, and tumbles,
And Silence sits in the banquet hall.

LOST AT SEA.

THE face that Carlo Dolci drew
Looks down from out its leafy hood —
The holly berries, gleaming through
The pointed leaves, seem drops of blood.

Above the cornice, round the hearth,
Are evergreens and spruce-tree boughs:
'T is Christmas morning: Christmas mirth
And joyous voices fill the house.

I pause, and know not what to do;
I feel reproach that I am glad:
Until to-day, no thought of you,
O Comrade! ever made me sad.

But now the thought of your blithe heart,
Your ringing laugh, can give me pain,
Knowing that we are worlds apart,
Not knowing we shall meet again.

For all is dark that lies in store:
Though they may preach, the brotherhood,
We know just this, and nothing more,
That we are dust, and God is good.

What life begins when death makes end?
Sleek gownsmen, is 't so very clear?
How fares it with us? — O, my Friend,
I only know you are not here!

That I am in a warm, light room,
With life and love to comfort me,
While you are drifting through the gloom,
Beneath the sea, beneath the sea!

O wild green waves that lash the sands
Of Santiago and beyond,
Lift him, I pray, with gentle hands,
And bear him on — true heart and fond!

To some still grotto far below
The washings of the warm Gulf Stream
Bear him, and let the winds that blow
About the world not break his dream!

— I smooth my brow. Upon the stair
I hear my children shout in glee,
With sparkling eyes and floating hair,
Bringing a Christmas wreath for me.

Their joy, like sunshine deep and broad,
Falls on my heart, and makes me glad:
I think the face of our dear Lord
Looks down on them, and seems not sad.

IN AN ATELIER.

I PRAY you, do not turn your head ;
And let your hands lie folded, so.
It was a dress like this, wine-red,
That Dante liked so, long ago.
You don't know Dante ? Never mind.
He loved a lady wondrous fair —
His model ? Something of the kind.
I wonder if she had your hair!

I wonder if she looked so meek,
And was not meek at all (my dear,
I want that side light on your cheek).
He loved her, it is very clear,
And painted her, as I paint you,
But rather better, on the whole
(Depress your chin: yes, that will do) :
He was a painter of the soul!

(And painted portraits, too, I think,
In the INFERNO — devilish good!
I 'd make some certain critics blink
If I 'd his method and his mood.)
Her name was (Fanny, let your glance
Rest there, by that majolica tray) —

Was Beatrice; they met by chance —
They met by chance, the usual way.

(As you and I met, months ago,
Do you remember? How your feet
Went crinkle-crinkle on the snow
Along the bleak gas-lighted street!
An instant in the drug-store's glare
You stood as in a golden frame,
And then I swore it, then and there,
To hand your sweetness down to fame.)

They met, and loved, and never wed
(All this was long before our time),
And though they died, they are not dead —
Such endless youth gives mortal rhyme!
Still walks the earth, with haughty mien,
Great Dante, in his soul's distress;
And still the lovely Florentine
Goes lovely in her wine-red dress.

You do not understand at all?
He was a poet; on his page
He drew her; and, though kingdoms fall,
This lady lives from age to age:
A poet — that means painter too,
For words are colors, rightly laid;
And they outlast our brightest hue,
For varnish cracks and crimsons fade.

The poets — they are lucky ones!
When *we* are thrust upon the shelves,

Our works turn into skeletons
Almost as quickly as ourselves;
For our poor canvas peels at length,
At length is prized — when all is bare:
"What grace!" the critics cry, "what strength!"
When neither strength nor grace is there.

Ah, Fanny, I am sick at heart,
It is so little one can do;
We talk our jargon — live for Art!
I 'd much prefer to live for you.
How dull and lifeless colors are!
You smile, and all my picture lies:
I wish that I could crush a star
To make a pigment for your eyes.

Yes, child, I know I 'm out of tune;
The light is bad; the sky is gray:
I paint no more this afternoon,
So lay your royal gear away.
Besides, you 're moody — chin on hand —
I know not what — not in the vein —
Not like Anne Bullen, sweet and bland:
You sit there smiling in disdain.

Not like Bluff Harry's radiant Queen,
Unconscious of the coming woe,
But rather as she might have been,
Preparing for the headsman's blow.
I see! I 've put you in a miff —
Sitting bolt-upright, wrist on wrist.
How *should* you look? Why, dear, as if —
Somehow — as if you 'd just been kissed!

THE QUEEN'S RIDE.

AN INVITATION.

'T IS that fair time of year,
  Lady mine,
When stately Guinevere,
In her sea-green robe and hood,
Went a-riding through the wood,
  Lady mine.

And as the Queen did ride,
  Lady mine,
Sir Launcelot at her side
Laughed and chatted, bending over,
Half her friend and all her lover,
  Lady mine.

And as they rode along,
  Lady mine,
The throstle gave them song,
And the buds peeped through the grass
To see youth and beauty pass,
  Lady mine.

And on, through deathless time,
  Lady mine,

9

These lovers in their prime.
(Two fairy ghosts together!)
Ride, with sea-green robe, and feather!
  Lady mine.

And so we two will ride.
  Lady mine,
At your pleasure, side by side.
Laugh and chat; I bending over,
Half your friend and all your lover,
  Lady mine.

But if you like not this.
  Lady mine,
And take my love amiss.
Then I 'll ride unto the end,
Half your lover, all your friend.
  Lady mine.

So, come which way you will.
  Lady mine,
Vale, upland, plain, and hill
Wait your coming. For one day
Loose the bridle, and away!
  Lady mine.

DIRGE.

Let us keep him warm,
Stir the dying fire:
Upon his tired arm
Slumbers young Desire.

Soon, ah, very soon
We too shall not know
Either sun or moon,
Either grass or snow.

Others in our place
Come to laugh and weep,
Win or lose the race,
And to fall asleep.

Let us keep him warm,
Stir the dying fire:
Upon his tired arm
Slumbers young Desire.

What does all avail —
Love, or power, or gold?
Life is like a tale
Ended ere 't is told.

Much is left unsaid,
Much is said in vain —
Shall the broken thread
Be taken up again?

Let us keep him warm,
Stir the dying fire:
Upon his tired arm
Slumbers young Desire.

Kisses one or two
On his eyelids set,
That, when all is through,
He may not forget.

He has far to go —
Is it East or West?
Whither? Who may know!
Let him take his rest.

Wind, and snow, and sleet —
So the long night dies.
Draw the winding-sheet,
Cover up his eyes.

Let us keep him warm,
Stir the dying fire:
Upon his tired arm
Slumbers young Desire.

THE PIAZZA OF ST. MARK AT MIDNIGHT.

HUSHED is the music, hushed the hum of voices;
Gone is the crowd of dusky promenaders —
Slender-waisted, almond-eyed Venetians,
Princes and paupers. Not a single footfall
Sounds in the arches of the Procuratie.
One after one, like sparks in cindered paper,
Faded the lights out in the goldsmiths' windows.
Drenched with the moonlight lies the still Piazza.

Fair as the palace builded for Aladdin,
Yonder St. Mark uplifts its sculptured splendor —
Intricate fretwork, Byzantine mosaic,
Color on color, column upon column,
Barbaric, wonderful, a thing to kneel to!
Over the portal stand the four gilt horses,
Gilt hoof in air, and wide distended nostril,
Fiery, untamed, as in the days of Nero.
Skyward, a cloud of domes and spires and crosses;
Earthward, black shadows flung from jutting stone-
        work.
High over all the slender Campanile
Quivers, and seems a falling shaft of silver!

Hushed is the music, hushed the hum of voices,
From coigne and cornice and fantastic gargoyle,

At intervals the moan of dove or pigeon,
Fairly faint, floats off into the moonlight.
This, and the murmur of the Adriatic,
Lazily restless, lapping the mossed marble,
Staircase or buttress, scarcely break the stillness.
Deeper each moment seems to grow the silence,
Denser the moonlight in the still Piazza.
Hark ! on the Tower above the ancient gateway,
The twin bronze Vulcans, with their ponderous ham-
    mers,
Hammer the midnight on their brazen bell there !

THE METEMPSYCHOSIS.

ABOVE the petty passions of the crowd
I stand in frozen marble like a god,
Inviolate, and ancient as the moon.
The thing I am, and not the thing Man is,
Fills my deep dreaming. Let him moan and die;
For he is dust that shall be laid again :
I know my own creation was divine.
Strewn on the breezy continents I see
The veinèd shells and burnished scales which once
Enclosed my being — husks that had their use ;
I brood on all the shapes I must attain
Before I reach the Perfect, which is God.
And dream my dream, and let the rabble go ;
For I am of the mountains and the sea,
The deserts, and the caverns in the earth,
The catacombs and fragments of old worlds.

I was a spirit on the mountain-tops,
A perfume in the valleys, a simoom
On arid deserts, a nomadic wind
Roaming the universe, a tireless Voice.
I was ere Romulus and Remus were ;
I was ere Nineveh and Babylon ;
I was, and am, and evermore shall be,
Progressing, never reaching to the end.
  A hundred years I trembled in the grass,
The delicate trefoil that muffled warm
A slope on Ida; for a hundred years
Moved in the purple gyre of those dark flowers
The Grecian women strew upon the dead.
Under the earth, in fragrant glooms, I dwelt ;
Then in the veins and sinews of a pine
On a lone isle, where, from the Cyclades,
A mighty wind, like a leviathan,
Ploughed through the brine, and from those solitudes
Sent Silence, frightened. To and fro I swayed,
Drawing the sunshine from the stooping clouds.
Suns came and went, and many a mystic moon,
Orbing and waning, and fierce meteors,
Leaving their lurid ghosts to haunt the night.
I heard loud voices by the sounding shore,
The stormy sea-gods, and from fluted conchs
Wild music, and strange shadows floated by,
Some moaning and some singing. So the years
Clustered about me, till the hand of God
Let down the lightning from a sultry sky,
Splintered the pine and split the iron rock ;
And from my odorous prison-house a bird,
I in its bosom, darted: so we flew,

Turning the brittle edge of one high wave,
Island and tree and sea-gods left behind!

Free as the air from zone to zone I flew,
Far from the tumult to the quiet gates
Of daybreak: and beneath me I beheld
Vineyards, and rivers that like silver threads
Ran through the green and gold of pasture-lands,
And here and there a hamlet, a white rose,
And here and there a city, whose slim spires
And palace-roofs and swollen domes uprose
Like scintillant stalagmites in the sun;
I saw huge navies battling with a storm
By ragged reefs along the desolate coasts,
And lazy merchantmen, that crawled, like flies,
Over the blue enamel of the sea
To India or the icy Labradors.

A century was as a single day.
What is a day to an immortal soul?
A breath, no more. And yet I hold one hour
Beyond all price — that hour when from the sky
I circled near and nearer to the earth,
Nearer and nearer, till I brushed my wings
Against the pointed chestnuts, where a stream,
That foamed and chattered over pebbly shoals,
Fled through the briony, and with a shout
Leapt headlong down a precipice: and there,
Gathering wild-flowers in the cool ravine,
Wandered a woman more divinely shaped
Than any of the creatures of the air,
Or river-goddesses, or restless shades
Of noble matrons marvellous in their time
For beauty and great suffering: and I sung,

I charmed her thought, I gave her dreams, and then
Down from the dewy atmosphere I stole
And nestled in her bosom. There I slept
From moon to moon, while in her eyes a thought
Grew sweet and sweeter, deepening like the dawn —
A mystical forewarning! When the stream,
Breaking through leafless brambles and dead leaves,
Piped shriller treble, and from chestnut boughs
The fruit dropt noiseless through the autumn night,
I gave a quick, low cry, as infants do:
We weep when we are born, not when we die!
So was it destined; and thus came I here,
To walk the earth and wear the form of Man,
To suffer bravely as becomes my state,
One step, one grade, one cycle nearer God.

And knowing these things, can I stoop to fret,
And lie, and haggle in the market-place,
Give dross for dross, or everything for naught?
No! let me stand above the crowd, and sing,
Waiting with hope for that miraculous change
Which seems like sleep; and though I waiting starve,
I cannot kiss the idols that are set
By every gate, in every street and park;
I cannot fawn, I cannot soil my soul;
For I am of the mountains and the sea,
The deserts, and the caverns in the earth,
The catacombs and fragments of old worlds.

THORWALDSEN.

WE often fail by searching far and wide
For what lies close at hand. To serve our turn
We ask fair wind and favorable tide.
From the dead Danish sculptor let us learn
To make Occasion, not to be denied:
Against the sheer, precipitous mountain-side
Thorwaldsen carved his Lion at Lucerne.

IV.

FRIAR JEROME'S BEAUTIFUL BOOK, ETC.

FRIAR JEROME'S BEAUTIFUL BOOK,
ETC.

FRIAR JEROME'S BEAUTIFUL BOOK.

A. D. 1200.

THE Friar Jerome, for some slight sin,
Done in his youth, was struck with woe.
"When I am dead," quoth Friar Jerome,
"Surely, I think my soul will go
Shuddering through the darkened spheres,
Down to eternal fires below!
I shall not dare from that dread place
To lift mine eyes to Jesus' face,
Nor Mary's, as she sits adored
At the feet of Christ the Lord.
Alas! December's all too brief
For me to hope to wipe away
The memory of my sinful May!"
And Friar Jerome was full of grief
That April evening, as he lay
On the straw pallet in his cell.
He scarcely heard the curfew-bell
Calling the brotherhood to prayer;
But he arose, for 't was his care

Nightly to feed the hungry poor
That crowded to the Convent door.

His choicest duty it had been :
But this one night it weighed him down.
" What work for an immortal soul,
To feed and clothe some lazy clown?
Is there no action worth my mood,
No deed of daring, high and pure,
That shall, when I am dead, endure,
A well-spring of perpetual good?"

And straight he thought of those great tomes
With clamps of gold — the Convent's boast —
How they endured, while kings and realms
Past into darkness and were lost;
How they had stood from age to age,
Clad in their yellow vellum-mail,
'Gainst which the Paynim's godless rage,
The Vandal's fire, could naught avail :
Though heathen sword-blows fell like hail,
Though cities ran with Christian blood,
Imperishable they had stood!
They did not seem like books to him,
But Heroes, Martyrs, Saints — themselves
The things they told of, not mere books
Ranged grimly on the oaken shelves.

To those dim alcoves, far withdrawn,
He turned with measured steps and slow,
Trimming his lantern as he went ;
And there, among the shadows, bent

Above one ponderous folio,
With whose miraculous text were blent
Seraphic faces: Angels, crowned
With rings of melting amethyst;
Mute, patient Martyrs, cruelly bound
To blazing fagots; here and there,
Some bold, serene Evangelist,
Or Mary in her sunny hair;
And here and there from out the words
A brilliant tropic bird took flight;
And through the margins many a vine
Went wandering — roses, red and white,
Tulip, wind-flower, and columbine
Blossomed.   To his believing mind

10

These things were real, and the wind,
Blown through the mullioned window, took
Scent from the lilies in the book.

"Santa Maria!" cried Friar Jerome,
"Whatever man illumined this,
Though he were steeped heart-deep in sin,
Was worthy of unending bliss,
And no doubt hath it! Ah! dear Lord,
Might I so beautify Thy Word!
What sacristan, the convents through,
Transcribes with such precision? who
Does such initials as I do?
Lo! I will gird me to this work,
And save me, ere the one chance slips.
On smooth, clean parchment I 'll engross
The Prophet's fell Apocalypse;
And as I write from day to day,
Perchance my sins will pass away."

So Friar Jerome began his Book.
From break of dawn till curfew-chime
He bent above the lengthening page,
Like some rapt poet o'er his rhyme.
He scarcely paused to tell his beads,
Except at night; and then he lay
And tost, unrestful, on the straw,
Impatient for the coming day —
Working like one who feels, perchance,
That, ere the longed-for goal be won,
Ere Beauty bare her perfect breast,
Black Death may pluck him from the sun.

At intervals the busy brook,
Turning the mill-wheel, caught his ear ;
And through the grating of the cell
He saw the honeysuckles peer,
And knew 't was summer, that the sheep
In fragrant pastures lay asleep,
And felt, that, somehow, God was near.
In his green pulpit on the elm,
The robin, abbot of that wood,
Held forth by times ; and Friar Jerome
Listened, and smiled, and understood.

While summer wrapt the blissful land
What joy it was to labor so,
To see the long-tressed Angels grow
Beneath the cunning of his hand,
Vignette and tail-piece subtly wrought !
And little recked he of the poor
That missed him at the Convent door ;
Or, thinking of them, put the thought
Aside. "I feed the souls of men
Henceforth, and not their bodies !" — yet
Their sharp, pinched features, now and then,
Stole in between him and his Book,
And filled him with a vague regret.

Now on that region fell a blight :
The corn grew cankered in its sheath ;
And from the verdurous uplands rolled
A sultry vapor fraught with death —
A poisonous mist, that, like a pall,
Hung black and stagnant over all.

Then came the sickness — the malign,
Green-spotted terror called the Pest,
That took the light from loving eyes,
And made the young bride's gentle breast
A fatal pillow. Ah! the woe,
The crime, the madness that befell !
In one short night that vale became
More foul than Dante's inmost hell.
Men curst their wives; and mothers left
Their nursing babes alone to die,
And wantoned, singing, through the streets,
With shameless brow and frenzied eye ;
And senseless clowns, not fearing God —
Such power the spotted fever had —
Razed Cragwood Castle on the hill,
Pillaged the wine-bins, and went mad.
And evermore that dreadful pall
Of mist hung stagnant over all :
By day, a sickly light broke through
The heated fog, on town and field :
By night, the moon, in anger, turned
Against the earth its mottled shield.

Then from the Convent, two and two,
The Prior chanting at their head,
The monks went forth to shrive the sick,
And give the hungry grave its dead —
Only Jerome, he went not forth,
But hiding in his dusty nook,
" Let come what will, I must illume
The last ten pages of my Book ! "
He drew his stool before the desk.

And sat him down, distraught and wan,
To paint his daring masterpiece,
The stately figure of Saint John.
He sketched the head with pious care,
Laid in the tint, when, powers of Grace!
He found a grinning Death's-head there,
And not the grand Apostle's face!

Then up he rose with one long cry:
" 'T is Satan's self does this," cried he,
" Because I shut and barred my heart
When Thou didst loudest call to me!
O Lord, Thou know'st the thoughts of men,
Thou know'st that I did yearn to make
Thy Word more lovely to the eyes
Of sinful souls, for Christ his sake!
Nathless, I leave the task undone:
I give up all to follow Thee —
Even like him who gave his nets
To winds and waves by Galilee!"

Which said, he closed the precious Book
In silence, with a reverent hand;
And drawing his cowl about his face
Went forth into the Stricken Land.
And there was joy in heaven that day —
More joy o'er this forlorn old friar
Than over fifty sinless men
Who never struggled with desire!

What deeds he did in that dark town,
What hearts he soothed with anguish torn,

What weary ways of woe he trod,
Are written in the Book of God,
And shall be read at Judgment Morn.
The weeks crept on, when, one still day,
God's awful presence filled the sky,
And that black vapor floated by,
And lo! the sickness past away.
With silvery clang, by thorpe and town,
The bells made merry in their spires:
O God! to think the Pest is flown!
Men kissed each other on the street,
And music piped to dancing feet
The livelong night, by roaring fires!

Then Friar Jerome, a wasted shape —
For he had taken the Plague at last —
Rose up, and through the happy town,
And through the wintry woodlands, past
Into the Convent. What a gloom
Sat brooding in each desolate room!
What silence in the corridor!
For of that long, innumerous train
Which issued forth a month before
Scarce twenty had come back again!

Counting his rosary step by step,
With a forlorn and vacant air,
Like some unshriven churchyard thing,
The Friar crawled up the mouldy stair
To his damp cell, that he might look
Once more on his belovéd Book.

And there it lay upon the stand,
Open! — he had not left it so.
He grasped it, with a cry; for, lo!
He saw that some angelic hand,
While he was gone, had finished it!
There 't was complete, as he had planned ;
There, at the end, stood ꞙinis, writ
And gilded as no man could do —
Not even that pious anchoret,
Bilfrid, the wonderful, nor yet
The miniatore Ethelwold,
Nor Durham's Bishop, who of old
(England still hoards the priceless leaves)
Did the Four Gospels all in gold.
And Friar Jerome nor spoke nor stirred,
But, with his eyes fixed on that word,
He passed from sin and want and scorn ;
And suddenly the chapel-bells
Rang in the holy Christmas-Morn!

In those wild wars which racked the land
Since then, and kingdoms rent in twain,
The Friar's Beautiful Book was lost —
That miracle of hand and brain :
Yet, though its leaves were torn and tost,
The volume was not writ in vain!

MIANTOWONA.

I.

Long ere the Pale Face
Crossed the Great Water,
Miantowona
Passed, with her beauty,
Into a legend
Pure as a wild-flower
Found in a broken
Ledge by the seaside.

Let us revere them —
These wildwood legends,
Born of the camp-fire.
Let them be handed
Down to our children —
Richest of heirlooms.
No land may claim them:
They are ours only,
Like our grand rivers,
Like our vast prairies,
Like our dead heroes.

II.

In the pine-forest,
Guarded by shadows,

Lieth the haunted
Pond of the Red Men.
Ringed by the emerald
Mountains, it lies there
Like an untarnished
Buckler of silver,
Dropped in that valley
By the Great Spirit!
Weird are the figures
Traced on its margins —
Vine-work and leaf-work,
Down-drooping fuchsias,
Knots of sword-grasses,
Moonlight and starlight,
Clouds scudding northward.
Sometimes an eagle
Flutters across it;
Sometimes a single
Star on its bosom
Nestles till morning.

Far in the ages,
Miantowona,
Rose of the Hurons,
Came to these waters.
Where the dank greensward
Slopes to the pebbles,
Miantowona
Sat in her anguish.
Ice to her maidens,
Ice to the chieftains,
Fire to her lover!

Here he had won her,
Here they had parted,
Here could her tears flow.
With unwet eyelash,
Miantowona
Nursed her old father,
Gray-eyed Tawanda,
Oldest of Hurons,
Soothed his complainings,
Smiled when he chid her
Vaguely for nothing —
He was so weak now,
Like a shrunk cedar
White with the hoar-frost.
Sometimes she gently
Linked arms with maidens,
Joined in their dances:
Not with her people,
Not in the wigwam,
Wept for her lover.

Ah! who was like him?
Fleet as an arrow,
Strong as a bison,
Lithe as a panther,
Soft as the south-wind,
Who was like Wawah?
There is one other
Stronger and fleeter,
Bearing no wampum,
Wearing no war-paint,
Ruler of councils,

Chief of the war-path —
Who can gainsay him,
Who can defy him?
His is the lightning,
His is the whirlwind,
Let us be humble,
We are but ashes —
'T is the Great Spirit!

Ever at nightfall
Miantowona
Strayed from the lodges,
Passed through the shadows
Into the forest:
There by the pond-side
Spread her black tresses
Over her forehead.
Sad is the loon's cry
Heard in the twilight;
Sad is the night-wind,
Moaning and moaning;
Sadder the stifled
Sob of a widow.

Low on the pebbles
Murmured the water:
Often she fancied
It was young Wawah
Playing the reed-flute.
Sometimes a dry branch
Snapped in the forest:
Then she rose, startled,

Ruddy as sunrise,
Warm for his coming !
But when he came not,
Back through the darkness,
Half broken-hearted,
Miantowona
Went to her people.

When an old oak dies,
First 't is the tree-tops,
Then the low branches,
Then the gaunt stem goes :
So fell Tawanda,
Oldest of Hurons,
Chief of the chieftains.

Miantowona
Wept not, but softly
Closed the sad eyelids ;
With her own fingers
Fastened the deer-skin
Over his shoulders :
Then laid beside him
Ash-bow and arrows,
Pipe-bowl and wampum,
Dried corn and bear-meat —
All that was needful
On the long journey.
Thus old Tawanda,
Went to the hunting
Grounds of the Red Man.

Then, as the dirges
Rose from the village,
Miantowona
Stole from the mourners,
Stole through the cornfields,
Passed like a phantom
Into the shadows
Through the pine-forest.

One who had watched her —
It was Nahoho,
Loving her vainly —
Saw, as she passed him,
That in her features
Made his stout heart quail.
He could but follow.
Quick were her footsteps,
Light as a snow-flake,
Leaving no traces
On the white clover.

Like a trained runner,
Winner of prizes,
Into the woodlands
Plunged the young chieftain.
Once he abruptly
Halted, and listened ;
Then he sped forward
Faster and faster
Toward the bright water.
Breathless he reached it.
Why did he crouch then,

Stark as a statue?
What did he see there

Could so appall him?
Only a circle
Swiftly expanding,
Fading before him;
But, as he watched it,
Up from the centre,
Slowly, superbly
Rose a Pond-Lily.

One cry of wonder,
Shrill as the loon's call,
Rang through the forest,
Startling the silence,
Startling the mourners

Chanting the death-song.
Forth from the village,
Flocking together
Came all the Hurons —
Striplings and warriors,
Maidens and old men,
Squaws with pappooses.
No word was spoken:
There stood the Hurons
On the dank greensward,
With their swart faces
Bowed in the twilight.
What did they see there?
Only a Lily
Rocked on the azure
Breast of the water.

Then they turned sadly
Each to the other,
Tenderly murmuring,
"Miantowona!"
Soft as the dew falls
Down through the midnight,
Cleaving the starlight,
Echo repeated,
"Miantowona!"

11

THE GUERDON.

Vedder, this legend if it had its due,
Would not be sung by me, but told by you
In colors such as Tintoretto knew.

Soothed by the fountain's drowsy murmuring —
Or was it by the west-wind's indolent wing? —
The grim court-poet fell asleep one day
In the lords' chamber, when chance brought that
      way
The Princess Margaret with a merry train
Of damozels and ladies — flippant, vain
Court-butterflies — midst whom fair Margaret
Swayed like a rathe and slender lily set
In rustling leaves, for all her drapery
Was green and gold, and lovely as could be.

Midway in hall the fountain rose and fell,
Filling a listless Naiad's outstretched shell
And weaving rainbows in the shifting light.
Upon the carven friezes, left and right,
Was pictured Pan asleep beside his reed.
In this place all things seemed asleep, indeed —
The hook-billed parrot on his pendent ring,
Sitting high-shouldered, half forgot to swing;
The wind scarce stirred the hangings at the door,

And from the silken arras evermore
Yawned drowsy dwarfs with satyr's face and hoof.

A forest of gold pillars propped the roof,
And like one slim gold pillar overthrown,
The sunlight through a great stained window shone
And lay across the body of Alain.
You would have thought, perchance, the man was
     slain:
As if the checkered column in its fall
Had caught and crushed him, he lay dead to all.
The parrot's gray bead eye as good as said,
Unclosing viciously, " The clown is dead."
A dragon-fly in narrowing circles neared,
And lit, secure, upon the dead man's beard.
Then spread its iris vans in quick dismay,
And into the blue summer sped away!

Little was his of outward grace to win
The eyes of maids, but white the soul within.
Misshaped, and hideous to look upon
Was this man, dreaming in the noontide sun,
With sunken eyes and winter-whitened hair,
And sallow cheeks deep seamed with thought and
     care.
And so the laughing ladies of the court,
Coming upon him suddenly, stopped short,
And shrunk together with a nameless dread;
Some, but fear held them, would have turned and
     fled,
Seeing the uncouth figure lying there.
But Princess Margaret, with her heavy hair

From out its diamond fillet rippling down,
Slipped from the group, and plucking back her
    gown
With white left hand, stole softly to his side —
The fair court gossips staring, curious-eyed,
Half mockingly. A little while she stood,
Finger on lip ; then, with the agile blood
Climbing her cheek, and silken lashes wet —
She scarce knew what vague pity or regret
Wet them — she stooped, and for a moment's space
Her golden tresses touched the sleeper's face.
Then she stood straight, as lily on its stem,
But hearing her ladies titter, turned on them
Her great queen's eyes, grown black with scornful
    frown —
Great eyes that looked the shallow women down.
" Nay, not for love " — one rosy palm she laid
Softly against her bosom — "as I 'm a maid!
Full well I know what cruel things you say
Of this and that, but hold your peace to-day.
I pray you think no evil thing of this.
Nay, not for love's sake did I give the kiss,
Not for his beauty who 's nor fair nor young,
But for the songs which those mute lips have sung! '

That was a right brave princess, one, I hold,
Worthy to wear a crown of beaten gold.

TITA'S TEARS.

A FANTASY.

A CERTAIN man of Ischia — it is thus
The story runs — one Lydus Claudius,
After a life of threescore years and ten,
Passed suddenly from out the world of men
Into the world of shadows.
               In a vale
Where shoals of spirits against the moonlight pale
Surged ever upward, in a wan-lit place
Near heaven, he met a Presence face to face —
A figure like a carving on a spire,
Shrouded in wings and with a fillet of fire
About the brows — who stayed him there, and said:
"This the gods grant to thee, O newly dead!
Whatever thing on earth thou holdest dear
Shall, at thy bidding, be transported here,
Save wife or child, or any living thing."
Then straightway Claudius fell to wondering
What he should wish for. Having heaven at hand,
His wants were few, as you can understand.
Riches and titles, matters dear to us,
To him, of course, were now superfluous:
But Tita, small brown Tita, his young wife,
A two weeks' bride when he took leave of life,

What would become of her without his care?
Tita, so rich, so thoughtless, and so fair!
At present crushed with sorrow, to be sure —
But by and by? What earthly griefs endure?
They pass like joys. A year, three years at most,
And would she mourn her lord, so quickly lost?
With fine, prophetic ear, he heard afar
The tinkling of some horrible guitar
Under her balcony. "Such thing could be,"
Sighed Claudius; "I would she were with me,
Safe from all harm." But as that wish was vain,
He let it drift from out his troubled brain
(His highly trained austerity was such
That self-denial never cost him much),
And strove to think what object he might name
Most closely linked with the bereavéd dame.
Her wedding ring? — 't would be too small to wear;
Perhaps a ringlet of her raven hair?
If not, her portrait, done in cameo,
Or on a background of pale gold? But no,
Such trifles jarred with his severity.
At length he thought: "The thing most meet for
        me
Would be that antique flask wherein my bride
Let fall her heavy tears the night I died."
(It was a custom of that simple day
To have one's tears sealed up and laid away,
As everlasting tokens of regret —
They find the bottles in Greek ruins yet.)
For this he wished, then.
                    Swifter than a thought
The Presence vanished, and the flask was brought —

Slender, bell-mouthed, and painted all around
With jet-black tulips on a saffron ground;
A tiny jar, of porcelain if you will,
Which twenty tears would rather more than fill.
With careful fingers Claudius broke the seal
When, suddenly, a well-known merry peal
Of laughter leapt from out the vial's throat,
And died, as dies the wood-bird's distant note.
Claudius stared; then, struck with strangest fears,
Reversed the flask —

        Alas, for Tita's tears!

THE LADY OF CASTELNORE.

A. D. 1700.

1.

BRÉTAGNE had not her peer. In the Province far
    or near
There were never such brown tresses, such a fault-
    less hand;
She had youth, and she had gold, she had jewels all
    untold,
And many a lover bold wooed the Lady of the
    Land.

2.

But she, with queenliest grace, bent low her pallid
    face,
And "Woo me not, for Jesus' sake, fair gentle-
    men," she said.

If they woo'd, then — with a frown she would strike
    their passion down :
She might have wed a crown to the ringlets on her
    head.

3.

From the dizzy castle-tips, hour by hour she watched
    the ships,
Like sheeted phantoms coming and going evermore,
While the twilight settled down on the sleepy sea-
    port town,
On the gables peaked and brown, that had sheltered
    kings of yore.

4.

Dusky belts of cedar-wood partly claspt the widen-
    ing flood ;
Like a knot of daisies lay the hamlets on the hill ;
In the hostelry below sparks of light would come
    and go,
And faint voices, strangely low, from the garrulous
    old mill.

5.

Here the land in grassy swells gently broke; there
    sunk in dells
With mosses green and purple, and prongs of rock
    and peat ;
Here, in statue-like repose, an old wrinkled mountain
    rose,
With its hoary head in snows, and wild-roses at its
    feet.

6.

And so oft she sat alone in the turret of gray stone,
And looked across the moorland, so woful, to the
    sea,
That there grew a village-cry, how her cheek did
    lose its dye,
As a ship, once, sailing by, faded on the sapphire
    lea.

7.

Her few walks led all one way, and all ended at the
    gray
And ragged, jagged rocks that fringe the lonely beach ;

There she would stand, the Sweet! with the white
    surf at her feet,
While above her wheeled the fleet sparrow-hawk with
    startling screech.

8.

And she ever loved the sea, with its haunting mys-
    tery,
Its whispering weird voices, its never-ceasing roar:
And 't was well that, when she died, they made her
    a grave beside
The blue pulses of the tide, by the towers of Castel-
    nore.

9.

Now, one chill November morn, many russet autumns
    gone,
A strange ship with folded wings lay dozing off the
    lea;
It had lain throughout the night with its wings of
    murky white
Folded, after weary flight — the worn nursling of
    the sea.

10.

Crowds of peasants flocked the sands; there were
    tears and clasping hands;
And a sailor from the ship stalked through the
    church-yard gate.
Then amid the grass that crept, fading, over her
    who slept,
How he hid his face and wept, crying. *Late, alas!*
    too late!

11.

And they called her cold. God knows . . . Under-
    neath the winter snows
The invisible hearts of flowers grow ripe for blossom-
    ing!
And the lives that look so cold, if their stories could
    be told,
Would seem cast in gentler mould, would seem full
    of love and spring.

THE TRAGEDY.

LA DAME AUX CAMÉLIAS.

La Dame aux Camélias —
    I think that was the play;
The house was packed from pit to dome
    With the gallant and the gay,
Who had come to see the Tragedy,
    And while the hours away.

There was the ruined Spendthrift,
    And Beauty in her prime;
There was the grave Historian,
    And there the man of Rhyme,
And the surly Critic, front to front,
    To see the play of crime.

And there was pompous Ignorance,
    And Vice in flowers and lace;

Sir Crœsus and Sir Pandarus —
  And the music played apace.
But of all that crowd I only saw
  A single, single face!

That of a girl whom I had known
  In the summers long ago,
When her breath was like the new-mown hay,
  Or the sweetest flowers that grow ;
When her heart was light, and her soul was white
  As the winter's driven snow.

And there she sat with her great brown eyes,
  They wore a troubled look ;
And I read the history of her life
  As it were an open book ;
And saw her Soul, like a slimy thing
  In the bottom of a brook.

There she sat in her rustling silk,
  With diamonds on her wrist,
And on her brow a gleaming thread
  Of pearl and amethyst.
" A cheat, a gilded grief ! " I said,
  And my eyes were filled with mist.

I could not see the players play :
  I heard the music moan :
It moaned like a dismal autumn wind.
  That dies in the woods alone ;
And when it stopped I heard it still —
  The mournful monotone !

What if the Count were true or false?
  I did not care, not I;
What if Camille for Armand died?
  I did not see her die.
There sat a woman opposite
  With piteous lip and eye!

The great green curtain fell on all,
  On laugh, and wine, and woe,
Just as death some day will fall
  'Twixt us and life, I know!
The play was done, the bitter play,
  And the people turned to go.

And did they see the Tragedy?
  They saw the painted scene;
They saw Armand, the jealous fool,
  And the sick Parisian queen:
But they did not see the Tragedy —
  The one I saw, I mean!

They did not see that cold-cut face,
  That furtive look of care;
Or, seeing her jewels, only said,
  " The lady 's rich and fair."
But I tell you, 't was the Play of Life,
  And that woman played Despair!

I.

Looking at Fra Gervasio,
Wrinkled and withered and old and gray,
A dry Franciscan from crown to toe,
You would never imagine, by any chance,
That, in the convent garden one day,
He spun this thread of golden romance.

Romance to me, but to him, indeed,
'T was a matter that did not hold a doubt:
A miracle, nothing more nor less.
Did I think it strange that, in our need,
Leaning from Heaven to our distress,
The Virgin brought such things about —
Gave mute things speech, made dead things move? —
Mother of Mercy, Lady of Love!
Besides, I might, if I wished, behold
The Bambino's self in his cloth of gold
And silver tissue, lying in state
In the Sacristy. Would the signor wait?

Whoever will go to Rome may see,
In the chapel of the Sacristy
Of Ara-Coeli, the Sainted Child —

Garnished from throat to foot with rings
And brooches and precious offerings,
And its little nose kissed quite away
By dying lips. At Epiphany,
If the holy winter day prove mild,
It is shown to the wondering, gaping crowd
On the church's steps — held high aloft —
While every sinful head is bowed,
And the music plays, and the censers' soft
White breath ascends like silent prayer.

Many a beggar kneeling there,
Tattered and hungry, without a home,
Would not envy the Pope of Rome,
If he, the beggar, had half the care
Bestowed on *him* that falls to the share
Of yonder Image — for you must know
It has its minions to come and go,
Its perfumed chamber, remote and still,

Its silken couch, and its jewelled throne,
And a special carriage of its own
To take the air in, when it will;
And though it may neither drink nor eat,
By a nod to its ghostly seneschal
It could have of the choicest wine and meat.
Often some princess, brown and tall,
Comes, and unclasping from her arm
The glittering bracelet, leaves it, warm
With her throbbing pulse, at the Baby's feet.
Ah, he is loved by high and low,
Adored alike by simple and wise.
The people kneel to him in the street.
What a felicitous lot is his —
To lie in the light of ladies' eyes,
Petted and pampered, and never to know
The want of a dozen *soldi* or so!
And what does he do for all of this?
What does the little Bambino do?
It cures the sick, and, in fact, 't is said
Can almost bring life back to the dead.
Who doubts it? Not Fra Gervasio.
When one falls ill, it is left alone
For a while with one — and the fever 's gone!

At least, 't was once so; but to-day
It is never permitted, unattended
By monk or priest, to work its lure
At sick folks' beds — all that was ended
By one poor soul whose feeble clay
Satan tempted and made secure.

It was touching this very point the friar
Told me the legend, that afternoon,
In the cloisteral garden all on fire
With scarlet poppies and golden stalks.
Here and there on the sunny walks,
Startled by some slight sound we made,
A lizard, awaking from its swoon,
Shot like an arrow into the shade.
I can hear the fountain's languorous tune,
(How it comes back, that hour in June
When just to exist was joy enough!)
I can see the olives, silvery-gray,
The carven masonry rich with stains,
The gothic windows with lead-set panes,
The flag-paved cortile, the convent grates,
And Fra Gervasio holding his snuff
In a squirrel-like meditative way
'Twixt finger and thumb. But the Legend waits.

II.

It was long ago (so long ago
That Fra Gervasio did not know
What year of our Lord), there came to Rome
Across the Campagna's flaming red,
A certain Filippo and his wife —
Peasants, and very newly wed.
In the happy spring and blossom of life,
When the light heart chirrups to lovers' calls,
These two, like a pair of birds, had come
And built their nest 'gainst the city's walls.

12

He, with his scanty garden-plots,
Raised flowers and fruit for the market-place,
Where she, with her pensile, flower-like face —
Own sister to her forget-me-nots —
Played merchant: and so they thrived apace,
In humble content, with humble cares
And modest longings, till, unawares,
Sorrow crept on them ; for to their nest
Had come no little ones, and at last,
When six or seven summers had past,
Seeing no baby at her breast,
The husband brooded, and then grew cold ;
Scolded and fretted over this —
Who would tend them when they were old,
And palsied, maybe, sitting alone,
Hungry, beside the cold hearth-stone ?
Not to have children, like the rest !
It cankered the very heart of bliss.

Then he fell into indolent ways,
Neglecting the garden for days and days,
Playing at *mora*, drinking wine,
With this and that one — letting the vine
Run riot and die for want of care,
And the choke-weeds gather : for it was spring,
When everything needed nurturing.
But he would drowse for hours in the sun,
Or sit on the broken step by the shed,
Like a man whose honest toil is done,
Sullen, with never a word to spare.
Or a word that were better all unsaid.

And Nina, so light of thought before,
Singing about the cottage door
In her mountain dialect — sang no more;
But came and went, sad-faced and shy,
Wishing, at times, that she might die,
Brooding and fretting in her turn.
Often, in passing along the street,
Her basket of flowers poised, peasant-wise,
On a lustrous braided coil of her hair,
She would halt, and her dusky cheek would burn
Like a poppy, beholding at her feet
Some stray little urchin, dirty and bare.
And sudden tears would spring to her eyes
That the tiny waif was not her own,
To fondle, and kiss, and teach to pray.
Then she passed onward, making moan.
Sometimes she would stand in the sunny square,
Like a slim bronze statue of Despair,
Watching the children at their play.

In the broad piazza was a shrine,
With Our Lady holding on her knee
A small nude waxen effigy.
Nina passed by it every day,
And morn and even, in rain or shine,
Repeated an *ave* there.   " Divine
Mother," she 'd cry, as she turned away,
" Sitting in paradise, undefiled,
O, have pity on my distress ! "
Then glancing back at the rosy Child,
She would cry to it, in her helplessness,
" Pray her to send the like to me ! "

Now once as she knelt before the saint,
Lifting her hands in silent pain,
She paled, and her heavy heart grew faint
At a thought which flashed across her brain —
The blinding thought that, perhaps if she
Had lived in the world's miraculous morn,
God might have chosen *her* to be
The mother — O heavenly ecstasy! —
Of the little babe in the manger born!
She, too, was a peasant girl, like her,
The wife of the lowly carpenter!
Like Joseph's wife, a peasant girl!

Her strange little head was in a whirl
As she rose from her knees to wander home,
Leaving her basket at the shrine ;
So dazed was she, she scarcely knew
The old familiar streets of Rome,
Nor whither she wished to go, in fine :
But wandered on, now crept, now flew,
In the gathering twilight, till she came
Breathless, bereft of sense and sight,
To the gloomy Arch of Constantine,
And there they found her, late that night,
With her cheeks like snow and her lips like flame!

Many a time from day to day,
She heard, as if in a troubled dream,
Footsteps around her, and some one saying —
Was it Filippo? — "Is she dead?"
Then it was some one near her praying,
And she was drifting — drifting away

From saints and martyrs in endless glory!
She seemed to be floating down a stream,
Yet knew she was lying in her bed.
The fancy held her that she had died,
And this was her soul in purgatory,
Until, one morning, two holy men
From the convent came, and laid at her side
The Bambino. Blessed Virgin! then
Nina looked up, and laughed, and wept,
And folded it close to her heart, and slept.

Slept such a soft, refreshing sleep,
That when she awoke her eyes had taken
The hyaline lustre, dewy, deep,
Of violets when they first awaken;
And the half-unravelled, fragile thread
Of life was knitted together again.
But she shrunk with sudden, strange new pain,
And seemed to droop like a flower, the day
The Capuchins came, with solemn tread,
To carry the Miracle Child away!

III.

Ere spring in the heart of pansies burned,
Or the buttercup had loosed its gold,
Nina was busy as ever of old
With fireside cares; but was not the same,
For from the hour when she had turned
To clasp the Image the fathers brought
To her dying-bed, a single thought
Had taken possession of her brain:
A purpose, as steady as the flame

Of a lamp in some cathedral crypt,
Had lighted her on her bed of pain ;
The thirst and the fever, they had slipt
Away like visions, but this had stayed —
To have the Bambino brought again,
To have it, and keep it for her own !
That was the secret dream which made
Life for her now — in the streets, alone,
At night, and morning, and when she prayed.

How should she wrest it from the hand
Of the jealous Church ?   How keep the Child ?
Flee with it into some distant land —
Like mother Mary from Herod's ire ?
Ah, well, she knew not ; she only knew
It was written down in the Book of Fate
That she should have her heart's desire,
And very soon now, for of late,
In a dream, the little thing had smiled
Up in her face, with one eye's blue
Peering from underneath her breast,
Which the baby fingers had softly prest
Aside, to look at her !   Holy one !
But that should happen ere all was done.

Lying dark in the woman's mind —
Unknown, like a seed in fallow ground —
Was the germ of a plan, confused and blind
At first, but which, as the weeks rolled round,
Reached light, and flowered, — a subtile flower,
Deadly as nightshade.   In that same hour
She sought the husband and said to him,

With crafty tenderness in her eyes
And treacherous archings of her brows,
" Filippo, mio, thou lov'st me well?
Truly ?   Then get thee to the house
Of the long-haired Jew Ben Raphaim —
Seller of curious tapestries,
(Ah, he hath everything to sell !)
The cunning carver of images —
And bid him to carve thee to the life
A *bambinetto* like that they gave
In my arms, to hold me from the grave
When the fever pierced me like a knife.
Perhaps, if we set the image there
By the Cross, the saints would hear the prayer
Which in all these years they have not heard."
Then the husband went, without a word,
To the crowded Ghetto; for since the days
Of Nina's illness, the man had been
A tender husband — with lover's ways
Striving, as best he might, to wean
The wife from her sadness, and to bring
Back to the home whence it had fled
The happiness of that laughing spring
When they, like a pair of birds, had wed.

The image!   It was a woman's whim —
They were full of whims.   But what to him
Were a dozen pieces of silver spent,
If it made her happy?   And so he went
To the house of the Jew Ben Raphaim.
And the carver heard, and bowed, and smiled,
And fell to work as if he had known

The thought that lay in the woman's brain,
And somehow taken it for his own:
For even before the month was flown
He had carved a figure so like the Child
Of Ara-Cœli, you 'd not have told.
Had both been decked with jewel and chain
And dressed alike in a dress of gold,
Which was the true one of the twain.

When Nina beheld it first, her heart
Stood still with wonder. The skilful Jew
Had given the eyes the tender blue,
And the cheeks the delicate olive hue,
And the form almost the curve and line
Of the Image the good Apostle made
Immortal with his miraculous art,
What time the sculptor [1] dreamed in the shade
Under the skies of Palestine.
The bright new coins that clinked in the palm
Of the carver in wood were blurred and dim
Compared with the eyes that looked at him
From the low sweet brows, so seeming calm;
Then he went his way, and her joy broke free.
And Filippo smiled to hear Nina sing
In the old, old fashioned — carolling
Like a very thrush, with many a trill
And long-drawn, flute-like, honeyed note,
Till the birds in the farthest mulberry.

[1] According to the monastic legend, the *Santissimo Bambino* was carved by a pilgrim, out of a tree which grew on the Mount of Olives, and painted by St. Luke while the pilgrim was sleeping over his work.

Each outstretching its amber bill,
Answered her with melodious throat.

Thus sped two days ; but on the third
Her singing ceased, and there came a change
As of death on Nina ; her talk grew strange,
Then she sunk in a trance, nor spoke nor stirred ;
And the husband, wringing his hands, dismayed,
Watched by the bed ; but she breathed no word
That night, nor until the morning broke,
When she roused from the spell, and feebly laid
Her hand on Filippo's arm, and spoke :
" Quickly, Filippo ! get thee gone
To the holy fathers, and beg them send
The Bambino hither " — her cheeks were wan
And her eyes like coals — " O, go, my friend,
Or all is said ! " Through the morning's gray
Filippo hurried, like one distraught,
To the monks, and told his tale ; and they,
Straight after matins, came and brought
The Miracle Child, and went their way.

Once more in her arms was the Infant laid,
After these weary months, once more !
Yet the woman seemed like a thing of stone
While the dark-robed fathers knelt and prayed ;
But the instant the holy friars were gone
She arose, and took the broidered gown
From the Baby Christ, and the yellow crown
And the votive brooches and rings it wore,
Till the little figure, so gay before
In its princely apparel, stood as bare

As your ungloved hand.   With tenderest care,
At her feet, 'twixt blanket and counterpane,
She hid the Babe; and then, reaching down
To the coffer wherein the thing had lain,
Drew forth Ben Raphaim's manikin
In haste, and dressed it in robe and crown,
With lace and bawble and diamond-pin.
This finished, she turned to stone again,
And lay as one would have thought quite dead,
If it had not been for a spot of red
Upon either cheek.   At the close of day
The Capuchins came, with solemn tread,
And carried the false bambino away!

Over the vast Campagna's plain,
At sunset, a wind began to blow
(From the Apennines it came, they say),
Softly at first, and then to grow —
As the twilight gathered and hurried by —
To a gale, with sudden tumultuous rain
And thunder muttering far away.
When the night was come, from the blackened sky
The spear-tongued lightning slipped like a snake,
And the great clouds clashed, and seemed to shake
The earth to its centre.   Then swept down
Such a storm as was never seen in Rome
By any one living in that day.
Not a soul dared venture from his home,
Not a soul in all the crowded town.
Dumb beasts dropped dead, with terror, in stall;
Great chimney-stacks were overthrown,
And about the streets the tiles were blown

Like leaves in autumn. A fearful night,
With ominous voices in the air!
Indeed, it seemed like the end of all.
In the convent, the monks for very fright
Went not to bed, but each in his cell
Counted his beads by the taper's light,
Quaking to hear the dreadful sounds,
And shrivelling in the lightning's glare.
It appeared as if the rivers of Hell
Had risen, and overleaped their bounds.

In the midst of this, at the convent door,
Above the tempest's raving and roar
Came a sudden knocking! Mother of Grace,
What desperate wretch was forced to face
Such a night as that was out-of-doors?
Across the echoless, stony floors
Into the windy corridors
The monks came flocking, and down the stair,
Silently, glancing each at each,
As if they had lost the power of speech.
Yes — it was some one knocking there!
And then — strange thing! — untouched by a soul
The bell of the convent 'gan to toll!
It curdled the blood beneath their hair.

Reaching the court, the brothers stood
Huddled together, pallid and mute,
By the massive door of iron-clamped wood,
Till one old monk, more resolute
Than the others — a man of pious will —
Stepped forth, and letting his lantern rest

On the pavement, crouched upon his breast
And peeped through a chink there was between
The cedar door and the sunken sill.
At the instant a flash of lightning came,
Seeming to wrap the world in flame.
He gave but a glance, and straight arose
With his face like a corpse's. What had he seen?
Two dripping, little pink-white toes!
Then, like a man gone suddenly wild,
He tugged at the bolts, flung down the chain,
And there, in the night and wind and rain —
Shivering, piteous, and forlorn,
And naked as ever it was born —
On the threshold stood the SAINTED CHILD!

" Since then," said Fra Gervasio,
" We have never let the Bambino go
Unwatched — no, not by a prince's bed.
Ah, signor, it made a dreadful stir."
" And the woman — Nina — what of her?
. Had she no story?" He bowed his head,
And knitting his meagre fingers, so —
" In that night of wind and wrath," said he,
" There was wrought in Rome a mystery.
What know I, signor? They found her dead!"

JUDITH.

I.

JUDITH IN THE TOWER.

Now Holofernes with his barbarous hordes
Crost the Euphrates, laying waste the land
To Esdraelon, and, falling on the town
Of Bethulia, stormed it night and day
Incessant, till within the leaguered walls
The boldest captains faltered; for at length
The wells gave out, and then the barley failed,
And Famine, like a murderer masked and cloaked,
Stole in among the garrison. The air
Was filled with lamentation, women's moans
And cries of children; and at night there came
A fever, parching as a fierce simoom.
Yet Holofernes could not batter down
The brazen gates, nor make a single breach
With beam or catapult in those tough walls:
And white with rage among the tents he strode,
Among the squalid Tartar tents he strode,
And curst the gods that gave him not his will,
And curst his captains, curst himself, and all;
Then, seeing in what strait the city was,
Withdrew his men hard by the fated town

Amid the hills, and with a grim-set smile
Waited, aloof, until the place should fall.
All day the house-top lay in sweltering heat,
All night the watch-fires flared upon the towers;
And day and night with Israelitish spears
The ramparts bristled.

             In a tall square Tower,
Full-fronting on the vile Assyrian camp,
Sat Judith, pallid as the cloudy moon
That hung half-faded in the dreary sky;
And ever and anon she turned her eyes
To where, between two vapor-haunted hills,
The dreadful army like a caldron seethed.
She heard, far off, the camels' gurgling groan,
The clank of arms, the stir and buzz of camps;
Beheld the camp-fires, flaming fiends of night
That leapt, and with red hands clutched at the
        dark ;
And now and then, as some mailed warrior stalked
Athwart the fires, she saw his armor gleam.
Beneath her stretched the temples and the tombs,
The city sickening of its own thick breath,
And over all the sleepless Pleiades.

  A star-like face, with floating clouds of hair —
Merari's daughter, dead Manasses' wife,
Who (since the barley-harvest when he died),
By holy charities, and prayers, and fasts,
Walked with the angels in her widow's weeds,
And kept her pure in honor of the dead.
But dearer to her bosom than the dead

Was Israel, its Prophets and its God:
And that dread midnight in the Tower alone,
Believing He would hear her from afar,
She lifted up the voices of her soul
Above the wrangling voices of the world:

"Oh, are we not Thy children who of old
Trod the Chaldean idols in the dust,
And built our altars only unto Thee?
   Didst Thou not lead us unto Canaan
For love of us, because we spurned the gods?
Didst Thou not bless us that we worshipped Thee?
   And when a famine covered all the land,
And drove us unto Egypt, where the King
Did persecute Thy chosen to the death —
   Didst Thou not smite the swart Egyptians then,
And guide us through the bowels of the deep
That swallowed up their horsemen and their King?
   For saw we not, as in a wondrous dream,
The up-tost javelins, the plunging steeds,
The chariots sinking in the wild Red Sea?
   O Lord, Thou hast been with us in our woe,
And from Thy bosom Thou hast cast us forth,
And to Thy bosom taken us again:
   For we have built our temples in the hills
By Sinai, and on Jordan's flowery banks,
And in Jerusalem we worship Thee.
   O Lord, look down and help us. Stretch Thy hand
And free Thy people. Make us pure in faith,
And draw us nearer, nearer unto Thee."

As when a harp-string trembles at a touch,
And music runs through all its quivering length.
And does not die, but seems to float away,
A silvery mist uprising from the string —
So Judith's prayer rose tremulous in the night,
And floated upward unto other spheres ;
And Judith loosed the hair about her brows,
And bent her head, and wept for Israel.

Now while she wept, bowed like a lotus-flower
That watches its own shadow in the Nile,
A stillness seemed to fall upon the land,
As if from out the calyx of a cloud,
That blossomed suddenly 'twixt the earth and moon.
It fell — and presently there came a sound
Of many pinions rustling in the dark,
And voices mingling, far and near, and strange
As sea-sounds on some melancholy coast
When first the equinox unchains the Storm.
And Judith started, and with one quick hand
Brushed back the plenteous tresses from a cheek
That whitened like a lily, and so stood,
Nor breathed, nor moved, but listened with her
        soul ;
And at her side, invisible, there leaned
An Angel mantled in his folded wings —
To her invisible, but other eyes
Beheld the saintly countenance ; for, lo !
Great clouds of spirits swoopt about the Tower
And drifted in the eddies of the wind.
The Angel stoopt, and from his radiant brow,
And from the gleaming amaranth in his hair,

A splendor fell on Judith, and she grew,
From her black tresses to her archéd feet,
Fairer than morning in Arabia.
Then silently the Presence spread his vans,
And rose — a luminous shadow in the air —
And through the zodiac, a white star, shot.

As one that wakens from a trance, she turned,
And heard the twilight twitterings of birds,
The wind in the turret, and from far below
Camp-sounds of pawing hoof and clinking steel;
And in the East she saw the early dawn
Breaking the night's enchantment; saw the Moon,
Like some wan sorceress, vanish in mid-heaven,
Leaving a moth-like glimmer where she died.
And Judith rose, and down the spiral stairs
Descended to the garden of the Tower,
Where, at the gate, lounged Achior, lately fled
From Holofernes; as she past she spoke :
"The Lord be with thee, Achior, all thy days."
And Achior saw the Spirit of the Lord
Had been with her, and, in a single night,
Worked such a miracle of form and face
As left her lovelier than all womankind
Who was before the fairest in Judæa.
But she, unconscious of God's miracle,
Moved swiftly on among a frozen group
Of statues that with empty, slim-necked urns
Taunted the thirsty Seneschal, until
She came to where, beneath the spreading palms,
Sat Chabris with Ozias and his friend
Charmis, governors of the leaguered town.

They saw a glory shining on her face
Like daybreak, and they marvelled as she stood
Bending before them with humility.
And wrinkled Charmis murmured through his beard:
" This woman walketh in the smile of God."

  " So walk we all," spoke Judith.   " Evermore
His light envelops us, and only those
Who turn aside their faces droop and die
In utter midnight.   If we faint we die.
O, is it true, Ozias, thou hast sworn
To yield our people to their enemies
After five days, unless the Lord shall stoop
From heaven to help us ? "

                      And Ozias said :
" Our young men die upon the battlements ;
Our wives and children by the empty tanks
Lie down and perish."

                  " If we faint we die.
The weak heart builds its palace on the sand,
The flood-tide eats the palace of a fool :
But whoso trusts in God, as Jacob did,
Though suffering greatly even to the end,
Dwells in a citadel upon a rock
That wind nor wave nor fire shall topple down."

  " Our young men die upon the battlements,"
Answered Ozias : " by the dusty wells
Our wives and children."

"They shall go and dwell
With Seers and Prophets in eternal joy!
Is there no God?"

"One only," Chabris spoke,
"But now His face is darkened in a cloud.
He sees not Israel."

"Is His mercy less
Than Holofernes'? Shall we place our faith
In this fierce bull of Assur? are we mad
That we so tear our throats with our own hands?"
And Judith's eyes flashed battle on the three,
Though all the woman quivered at her lip
Struggling with tears.

"In God we place our trust,"
Said old Ozias, "yet for five days more."

"Ah! His time is not man's time," Judith cried,
"And why should we, the dust about His feet,
Decide the hour of our deliverance,
Saying to Him, *Thus shalt Thou do, and so?*"

Then gray Ozias bowed his head, abashed
That eighty winters had not made him wise,
For all the drifted snow of his long beard:
"This woman speaketh wisely. We were wrong
That in our anguish mocked the Lord our God,
The staff, the scrip, the stream whereat we drink."
And then to Judith: "Child, what wouldst thou
    have?"

" I know and know not. Something I know not
Makes music in my bosom ; as I move
A presence goes before me, and I hear
New voices mingling in the upper air :
Within my hand there seems another hand
Close-prest, that leads me to yon dreadful camp;
While in my brain the fragments of a dream
Lie like a broken string of diamonds,
The choicest missing. Ask no more. I know
And know not. . . . . See ! the very air is white
With fingers pointing. Where they point I go."

She spoke and paused : the three old men looked
    up
And saw a sudden motion in the air
Of white hands waving : and they dared not speak,
But muffled their thin faces in their robes,
And sat like those grim statues which the wind
Near some unpeopled city in the East
From foot to forehead wraps in desert dust.

" Ere thrice the shadow of the temple slants
Across the fountain, I shall come again."
Thus Judith softly : then a gleam of light
Played through the silken lashes of her eyes,
As lightning through the purple of a cloud
On some still tropic evening, when the breeze
Lifts not a single blossom from the bough :
" What lies in that unfolded flower of time
No man may know. The thing I can I will,
Leaning on God, remembering how He loved
Jacob in Syria when he fed the flocks

Of Laban, and what miracles He did
For Abraham and for Isaac at their need.
Wait thou the end ; and, till I come, keep thou
The sanctuaries." And Ozias swore
By those weird fingers pointing in the air,
And by the soul of Abraham gone to rest,
To keep the sanctuaries, though she came
And found the bat sole tenant of the Tower,
And all the people bleaching on the walls,
And no voice left. Then Judith moved away,
Her head bowed on her bosom, like to one
That moulds some subtle purpose in a dream,
And in his passion rises up and walks
Through labyrinths of slumber to the dawn.

When she had gained her chamber she threw off
The livery of sorrow for her lord,
The cruel sackcloth that begirt her limbs,
And from those ashen colors issuing forth,
Seemed like a golden butterfly new-slipt
From its dull chrysalis. Then, after bath,
She braided in the darkness of her hair
A thread of opals; on her rounded breast
Spilt precious ointment; and put on the robes
Whose rustling made her pause, half-garmented,
To dream a moment of her bridal morn.
Of snow-white silk stuff were the robes, and rich
With delicate branch-work, silver-frosted star,
And many a broidered lily-of-the-vale.
These things became her as the scent the rose,
For fairest things are beauty's natural dower.
The sun that through the jealous casement stole

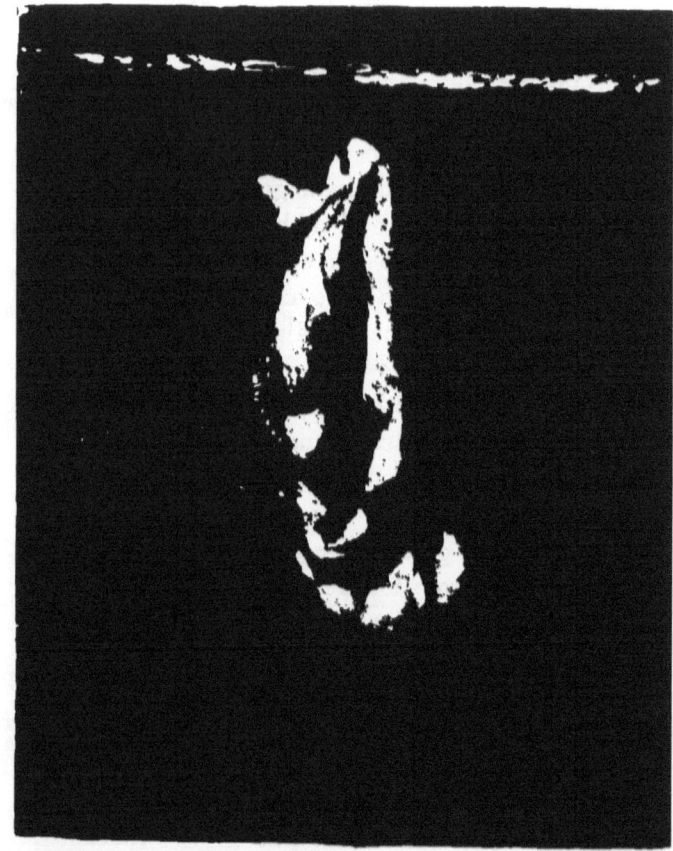

Fawned on the Hebrew woman as she stood,
Toyed with the oval pendant at her ear,
And, like a lover, stealing to her lips
Taught them a deeper crimson ; then slipt down
The tremulous lilies to the sandal straps
That bound her snowy ankles.

Forth she went,
A glittering wonder, through the crowded streets,
Her handmaid, like a shadow, following on.
And as in summer when the beaded wheat
Leans all one way, and with a longing look
Marks the quick convolutions of the wind,
So all eyes went with Judith as she moved,
All hearts leaned to her with a weight of love.
A starving woman lifted ghostly hands
And blest her for old charities; a child
Smiled on her through its tears; and one gaunt chief
Threw down his battle-axe and doffed his helm,
As if some bright Immortal swept him by.

So forth she fared, the only thing of light
In that dark city, thridding tortuous ways
By gloomy arch and frowning barbacan,
Until she reached a gate of triple brass
That opened at her coming, and swung to
With horrid clangor and a ring of bolts.
And there, outside the city of her love,
The warm blood at her pulses, Judith paused
And drank the morning; then with silent prayers
Moved on through flakes of sunlight, through the
        wood
To Holofernes and his barbarous hordes.

THE CAMP OF ASSUR.

As on the house-tops of a seaport town,
After a storm has lashed the dangerous coast,
The people crowd to watch some hopeless ship
Tearing its heart upon the unseen reef,
And strain their sight to catch the tattered sail
That comes and goes, and glimmers, till at last
No eye can find it, and a sudden awe
Falls on the people, and no soul may speak :
So, from the windy parapets and roofs
Of the embattled city, anxious groups
Watched the faint flutter of a woman's dress —
Judith, who, toiling up a distant hill,
Seemed but a speck against the sunny green :
Yet ever as the wind drew back her robes,
They saw her from the towers, until she reached
The crest, and past into the azure sky.
Then, each one gazing on his neighbor's face,
Speechless, descended to the level world.

Before his tent, stretched on a leopard-skin,
Lay Holofernes, ringed by his dark lords —
Himself the prince of darkness. At his side
His iron helmet poured upon the grass
Its plume of horsehair : on his ponderous spear,
The flinty barb thrust half its length in earth,

As if some giant had flung it, hung his shield,
And on the burnished circuit of the shield
A sinewy dragon, rampant, silver-fauged,
Glared horrible with sea-green emerald eyes ;
And, as the sunshine struck across it, writhed,
And seemed a type of those impatient lords
Who, in the loud war-council here convened,
Gave voice for battle, and with fiery words
Opposed the cautious wisdom of their peers.
So seemed the restless dragon on the shield.

Baleful and sullen as a sulphurous cloud
Packed with the lightning, Holofernes lay,
Brooding upon the diverse arguments,
Himself not arguing, but listening most
To the curt phrases of the gray-haired chiefs.
And some said: "Take the city by assault,
And grind it into atoms at a blow."
And some said : "Wait. There 's that within the
        walls
Shall gnaw its heart out — hunger. Let us wait."
To which the younger chieftains : "If we wait,
Ourselves shall starve. Like locusts we have fed
Upon the land till there is nothing left,
Nor grass, nor grain, nor any living thing.
And if at last we take a famished town
With fifty thousand ragged skeletons,
What boots it ? We shall hunger all the same.
Now, by great Baäl, we 'd rather die at once
Than languish, scorching, on these sun-baked hills!"
At which the others called them "fretful girls,"
And scoffed at them : "Ye should have stayed at
        home.

And decked your hair with sunny butterflies,
Like King Arphaxad's harlots. Know ye not
Patience and valor are the head and heart
Of warriors? Who lacks in either, fails.
Have we not hammered with our catapults
Those stubborn gates? Have we not hurled our
        men
Against the angry torrent of their spears?
Mark how those birds that wheel above yon wood,
In clanging columns, settle greedily down
Upon the unearthed bodies of our dead.
See where they rise, red-beaked and surfeited!
Has it availed? Let us be patient, then,
And bide the sovran pleasure of the gods."
"And when," quoth one, "our stores of meat are
        gone,
We 'll even feed upon the tender flesh
Of these tame girls, who, though they dress in steel,
Like more the dulcet tremors of a lute
Than the shrill whistle of an arrow-head."

At this a score of falchions leapt in air,
And hot-breathed words took flight from bearded
        lips,
And they had slain each other in their heat,
These savage captains, quick with bow and spear,
But that dark Holofernes started up
To his full height, and, speaking not a word,
With anger-knitted forehead glared at them.
As they shrunk back, their passion and their shame
Gave place to wonder, finding in their midst
A woman whose exceeding radiance

Of brow and bosom made her garments seem
Threadbare and lustreless, yet whose attire
Outshone the purples of a Persian queen.

For Judith, who knew all the mountain paths
As one may know the delicate azure veins,
Each crossing each, on his belovéd's wrist,
Had stolen between the archers in the wood
And gained the straggling outskirts of the camp,
And seeing the haughty gestures of the chiefs,
Halted, with fear, and knew not where to turn;
Then taking heart, had silently approached,
And stood among them, until then unseen.
And in the air, like numerous swarms of bees,
Arose the wondering murmurs of her throng,
Which checking, Holofernes turned and cried,
" Who breaks upon our councils?" angrily,
But drinking then the beauty of her eyes,
And seeing the rosy magic of her mouth,
And all the fragrant summer of her hair
Blown sweetly round her forehead, stood amazed;
And in the light of her pure modesty
His voice took gentler accent unawares:
" Whence come ye?"
                                    " From yon city."
                                                        " By our life,
We thought the phantom of some murdered queen
Had risen from dead summers at our feet!
If these Judæan women are so shaped,
Daughters of goddesses, let none be slain.
What seek ye, woman, in the hostile camps
Of Assur?"

" Holofernes."

" This is he."

" O good my lord," cried Judith, " if indeed
Thou art that Holofernes whom I seek,
And seeking dread to find, low at thy feet
Behold thy handmaid, who in fear has flown
From a doomed people."

" Wherein thou wert wise
Beyond the usual measure of thy sex,
And shalt have such observance as a king
Gives to his mistress, though our enemy.
As for thy people, they shall rue the hour
That brought not tribute to the lord of all,
Nabuchodonosor. But thou shalt live."

" O good my lord," spoke Judith, " as thou wilt.
So would thy handmaid; and I pray thee now
Let those that listen stand awhile aloof,
For I have that for thine especial ear
Most precious to thee." Then the crowd fell back,
Muttering, and half reluctantly, because
Her beauty drew them as the moon the sea —
Fell back and lingered, leaning on their shields
Under the trees, some couchant in the grass,
Broad-throated, large-lunged Titans overthrown,
Eying the Hebrew woman, whose sweet looks
Brought them a sudden vision of their wives
And longings for them : and her presence there
Was as a spring that, in Sahara's wastes,
Taking the thirsty traveller by surprise,
Loosens its silver music at his feet.
Then Judith, modest, with down-drooping eyes :

" My lord, if yet thou holdest in thy thought
The words which Achior the Ammonite
Once spake to thee concerning Israel,
O treasure them, for in them was no guile.
True is it, master, that our people kneel
To an unseen but not an unknown God :
By day and night He watches over us,
And while we worship Him we cannot die,
Our tabernacles shall be unprofaned,
Our spears invincible ; but if we sin,
If we transgress the law by which we live,
Our temples shall be desecrate, our tribes
Thrust forth into the howling wilderness,
Scourged and accurséd. Therefore, O my lord,
Seeing this nation wander from the faith
Taught of the Prophets, I have fled dismayed,
For fear the towers might crush me as they fall.
Heed, Holofernes, what I speak this day,
And if the thing I tell thee prove not true
Ere thrice the sun goes down beyond those peaks,
Then straightway plunge thy falchion in my breast,
For 't were not meet that thy handmaid should live,
Having deceived the crown and flower of men."

She spoke and paused : and sweeter on his ear
Were Judith's words than ever seemed to him
The wanton laughter of the Assyrian girls
In the bazaars ; and listening he heard not
The never-ceasing murmurs of the camp,
The neighing of the awful battle-steeds,
Nor the vain wind among the drowsy palms.
The tents that straggled up the hot hillsides,

14

The warriors lying in the tangled grass,
The fanes and turrets of the distant town,
And all that was, dissolved and past away,
Save this one woman with her twilight eyes
And the miraculous cadence of her voice.

Then Judith, catching at the broken thread
Of her discourse, resumed, to closer draw
The silken net about the foolish prince;
And as she spoke, from time to time her gaze
Dwelt on his massive stature, and she saw
That he was shapely, knitted like a god,
A tower beside the men of her own land.

"Heed, Holofernes, what I speak this day,
And thou shalt rule not only Bethulia,
Rich with its hundred altars' crusted gold,
But Cades-Barne, Jerusalem, and all
The vast hill-country even to the sea:
For I am come to give unto thy hands
The key of Israel, — Israel now no more,
Since she disowns her Prophets and her God.
Know then, O lord, it is our yearly use
To lay aside the first fruit of the grain,
And so much oil, so many skins of wine,
Which, being sanctified, are kept intact
For the High Priests who serve before our God
In the great temple at Jerusalem.
This holy food — which even to touch is death —
The rulers, sliding from their ancient faith,
Would fain lay hands on, being wellnigh starved:
And they have sent a runner to the Priests

(The Jew Ben Raphaim, who, at dead of night,
Shot like a javelin between thy guards),
Bearing a parchment begging that the Church
Yield them permit to eat the sacred corn.
But 't is not lawful they should do this thing,
Yet will they do it.   Then shalt thou behold
The archers tumbling headlong from the walls,
Their strength gone from them ; thou shalt see the
        spears
Splitting like reeds within the spearmen's hands,
And the pale captains tottering like old men
Stricken with palsy.   Then, O glorious prince,
Then with thy trumpets blaring doleful dooms,
And thy silk banners flapping in the wind,
With squares of men and eager clouds of horse
Thou shalt swoop down on them, and strike them
        dead !
But now, my lord, before this come to pass,
Three days must wane, for they touch not the food
Until the Jew Ben Raphaim shall return
With the Priests' message.   Here among thy hosts,
O Holofernes, will I dwell the while,
Asking but this, that I and my handmaid
Each night, at the twelfth hour, may egress have
Unto the valley, there to weep and pray
That God forsake this nation in its sin.
And as my prophecy prove true or false,
So be it with me."
                    Judith ceased, and stood,
Her hands across her bosom, as in prayer ;
And Holofernes answered : " Be it so.
And if, O pearl of women, the event

Prove not a dwarf beside the prophecy,
Then there 's no woman like thee — no, not one.
Thy name shall be renownéd through the world,
Music shall wait on thee, thou shalt have crowns,
And jewel-chests of costly camphor-wood,
And robes as glossy as the ring-dove's neck,
And milk-white mares, and chariots, and slaves:
And thou shalt dwell with me in Nineveh,
In Nineveh, the City of the Gods!"

At which the Jewish woman bowed her head
Humbly, that Holofernes might not see
How blanched her cheek grew. " Even as thou
        wilt,
So would thy servant." At a word the slaves
Brought meat and wine, and placed them in a
        tent,
A silk pavilion, wrought with arabesques,
That stood apart, for Judith and her maid.
But Judith ate not, saying: " Master, no.
It is not lawful that we taste of these;
My maid has brought a pouch of parchéd corn,
And bread, and figs, and wine of our own land,
Which shall not fail us." Holofernes said,
" So let it be," and lifting up the screen
Past out, and left them sitting in the tent.

That day he mixt not with the warriors
As was his wont, nor watched them at their games
In the wide shadow of the terebinth-trees;
But up and down within a lonely grove
Paced slowly, brooding on her perfect face,

Saying her smooth words over to himself,
Heedless of time, till he looked up and saw
The spectre of the Twilight on the hills.

The fame of Judith's loveliness had flown
From lip to lip throughout the canvas town,
And as the evening deepened, many came
From neighboring camps, with frivolous excuse,
To pass the green pavilion — long-haired chiefs
That dwelt by the Hydaspe, and the sons
Of the Elymeans, and slim Tartar youths ;
But saw not her, who, shut from common air,
Basked in the twilight of the tapestries.

But when night came, and all the camp was still,
And nothing moved beneath the icy stars
In their blue bourns, except some stealthy guard,
A shadow among shadows, Judith rose,
Calling her servant, and the sentinel
Drew back, and let her pass beyond the lines
Into the valley. And her heart was full,
Seeing the watch-fires burning on the towers
Of her own city: and she knelt and prayed
For it and them that dwelt within its walls,
And was refreshed — such balm there lies in prayer
For those who know God listens. Straightway then
The two returned, and all the camp was still.

One cresset twinkled dimly in the tent
Of Holofernes, and Bagoas, his slave,
Lay prone across the matting at the door,
Drunk with the wine of slumber; but his lord

Slept not, or, sleeping, rested not for thought
Of Judith's beauty. Two large lucent eyes,
Tender and full as moons, dawned on his sleep ;
And when he woke, they filled the vacant dusk
With an unearthly splendor. All night long
A stately figure glided through his dream ;
Sometimes a queenly diadem weighed down
Its braided tresses, and sometimes it came
Draped only in a misty cloud of veils,
Like the King's dancing-girls at Nineveh.
And once it bent above him in the gloom,
And touched his forehead with most hungry lips.
Then Holofernes turned upon his couch,
And, yearning for the daybreak, slept no more.

III

THE FLIGHT.

In the far east, as viewless tides of time
Drew on the drifting shallop of the Dawn,
A fringe of gold went rippling up the gray,
And breaking rosily on cliff and spur,
Still left the vale in shadow. While the fog
Folded the camp of Assur, and the dew
Yet shook in clusters on the new green leaf,
And not a bird had dipt a wing in air,
The restless captain, haggard with no sleep,
Stept over the curved body of his slave,
And thridding moodily the dingy tents,
Hives packed with sleepers, stood within the grove,
And in the cool, gray twilight gave his thought
Wings ; but however wide his fancies flew,
They circled still the figure of his dream.

He sat: before him rose the fluted domes
Of Nineveh, his city, and he heard
The clatter of the merchants in the booths
Selling their merchandise : and now he breathed
The airs of a great river, sweeping down
Past carven pillars, under tamarisk boughs,
To where the broad sea sparkled : then he groped
In a damp catacomb, he knew not where,
By torchlight, hunting for his own grim name

On some sarcophagus : and as he mused,
From out the ruined kingdom of the Past
Glided the myriad women he had wronged,
The half-forgotten passions of his youth ;
Dark-browed were some, with haughty, sultry eyes,
Imperious and most ferocious loves ;
And some, meek blondes with lengths of flaxen hair —
Daughters of Sunrise, shaped of fire and snow,
And Holofernes smiled a bitter smile
Seeing these spectres in his revery,
When suddenly one face among the train
Turned full upon him — such a piteous face,
Blanched with such anguish, looking such reproach,
So sunken-eyed and awful in its woe,
His heart shook in his bosom, and he rose
As if to smite it, and before him stood
Bagoas, the bondsman, bearing in his arms
A jar of water, while the morning broke
In dewy splendor all about the grove.

Then Holofernes, vext that he was cowed
By his own fantasy, strode back to camp,
Bagoas following, sullen, like a hound
That takes the color of his master's mood.
And with the troubled captain went the shapes
Which even the daylight could not exorcise.

"Go, fetch me wine, and let my soul make cheer,
For I am sick with visions of the night.
Some strangest malady of breast and brain
Hath so unnerved me that a rustling leaf
Sets my pulse leaping. 'T is a family flaw,

A flaw in men else flawless, this dark spell:
I do remember when my grandsire died,
He thought a lying Ethiop he had slain
Was strangling him; and, later, my own sire
Went mad with dreams the day before his death.
And I, too? Slave! go fetch me seas of wine,
That I may drown these fantasies — no, stay!
Ransack the camps for choicest flesh and fruit,
And spread a feast within my tent this night,
And hang the place with garlands of new flowers;
Then bid the Hebrew woman, yea or nay,
To banquet with us. As thou lov'st the light,
Bring her; and if indeed the gods have called,
The gods shall find me sitting at my feast
Consorting with a daughter of the gods!'"

Thus Holofernes, turning on his heel
Impatiently; and straight Bagoas went
And spoiled the camps of viands for the feast,
And hung the place with flowers, as he was bid;
And seeing Judith's servant at the well,
Gave his lord's message, to which answer came:
" O what am I that should gainsay my lord ? "
And Holofernes smiled within, and thought:
" Or life or death, if I should have her not
In spite of all, my mighty name would be
A word for laughter among womankind."

" So soon! " thought Judith. " Flying pulse, be
    still!
O Thou who lovest Israel, give me strength
And cunning such as never woman had,

That my deceit may be his stripe and scar,
My kisses his destruction. This for thee.
My city, Bethulîa, this for thee!"

　And thrice that day she prayed within her heart,
Bowed down among the cushions of the tent
In shame and wretchedness; and thus she prayed:
"O save me from him, Lord! but save me most
From mine own sinful self: for, lo! this man,
Though viler than the vilest thing that walks,
A worshipper of fire and senseless stone,
Slayer of children, enemy of God —
He, even he, O Lord, forgive my sin,
Hath by his heathen beauty moved me more
Than should a daughter of Judæa be moved,
Save by the noblest. Clothe me with Thy love,
And rescue me, and let me trample down
All evil thought, and from my baser self
Climb up to Thee, that aftertimes may say:
She tore the guilty passion from her soul, —
Judith the pure, the faithful unto death."

　Half seen behind the forehead of a crag
The evening-star grew sharp against the dusk,
As Judith lingered by the curtained door
Of her pavilion, waiting for Bagoas:
Erewhile he came, and led her to the tent
Of Holofernes: and she entered in,
And knelt before him in the cresset's glare
Demurely, like a slave-girl at the feet
Of her new master, while the modest blood
Makes protest to the eyelids; and he leaned

Graciously over her, and bade her rise
And sit beside him on the leopard-skins.
But Judith would not, yet with gentlest grace
Would not; and partly to conceal her blush,
Partly to quell the riot in her breast,
She turned, and wrapt her in her fleecy scarf,
And stood aloof, nor looked as one that breathed,
But rather like some jewelled deity
Taken by a conqueror from its sacred niche,
And placed among the trappings of his tent —
So pure was Judith.

      For a moment's space
She stood, then stealing softly to his side,
Knelt down by him, and with uplifted face,
Whereon the red rose blossomed with the white:
" This night, my lord, no other slave than I
Shall wait on thee with fruits and flowers and wine.
So subtle am I, I shall know thy wish
Ere thou canst speak it. Let Bagoas go
Among his people : let me wait and serve,
More happy as thy handmaid than thy guest."

Thereat he laughed, and, humoring her mood,
Gave the black bondsman freedom for the night.
Then Judith moved, obsequious, and placed
The meats before him, and poured out the wine,
Holding the golden goblet while he ate,
Nor ever past it empty ; and the wine
Seemed richer to him for those slender hands.
So Judith served, and Holofernes drank,
Until the lamps that glimmered round the tent
In mad processions danced before his gaze.

Without, the moon dropt down behind the sky;
Within, the odors of the heavy flowers,
And the aromas of the mist that curled
From swinging cressets, stole into the air:
And through the mist he saw her come and go,
Now showing a faultless arm against the light,
And now a dainty sandal set with gems.
At last he knew not in what place he was,
For as a man who, softly held by sleep,
Knows that he dreams, yet knows not true from
  false,
Perplext between the margins of two worlds,
So Holofernes, flushed with the red wine,

Like a bride's eyes, the eyes of Judith shone,
As ever bending over him with smiles
She filled the generous chalice to the edge;
And half he shrunk from her, and knew not why,
Then wholly loved her for her loveliness,
And drew her close to him, and breathed her
  breath:
And once he thought the Hebrew woman sang
A wine-song, touching on a certain king
Who, dying of strange sickness, drank, and past
Beyond the touch of mortal agony —
A vague tradition of the cunning sprite
That dwells within the circle of the grape,
And thus he heard, or fancied that he heard: —

The small green grapes in countless clusters grew,
Feeding on mystic moonlight and white dew
And mellow sunshine, the long summer through:

Till, with faint tremor in her veins, the Vine
Felt the delicious pulses of the wine ;
And the grapes ripened in the year's decline.

And day by day the Virgins watched their charge ;
And when, at last, beyond the horizon's marge,
The harvest-moon droopt beautiful and large,

The subtle spirit in the grape was caught,
And to the slowly dying Monarch brought,
In a great cup fantastically wrought,

Whereof he drank ; then straightway from his brain
Went the weird malady, and once again
He walked the Palace, free of scar or pain —

But strangely changed, for somehow he had lost
Body and voice : the courtiers, as he crost
The royal chambers, whispered — *The King's Ghost!*

"A potent medicine for kings and men,"
Thus Holofernes ; "he was wise to drink.
Be thou as wise, fair Judith."   As he spoke,
He stoopt to kiss the treacherous soft hand
That rested like a snow-flake on his arm,
But stooping reeled, and from the place he sat
Toppled, and fell among the leopard-skins :
There lay, nor stirred ; and ere ten beats of heart,
The tawny giant slumbered.

     Judith knelt
And gazed upon him, and her thoughts were dark ;

For half she longed to bid her purpose die —
To stay, to weep, to fold him in her arms,
To let her long hair loose upon his face,
As on a mountain-top some amorous cloud
Lets down its sombre tresses of fine rain.
For one wild instant in her burning arms
She held him sleeping ; then grew wan as death,
Relaxed her hold, and starting from his side
As if an asp had stung her to the quick,
Listened ; and listening, she heard the moans
Of little children moaning in the streets
Of Bethulia, saw famished women pass,
Wringing their hands, and on the broken walls
The flower of Israel dying.

                      With quick breath
Judith blew out the tapers, all save one,
And from his twisted girdle loosed the sword,
And grasping the huge hilt with her two hands,
Thrice smote the Prince of Assur as he lay,
Thrice on his neck she smote him as he lay,
And from the brawny shoulders rolled the head
Winking and ghastly in the cresset's light :
Which done, she fled into the yawning dark,
There met her maid, who, stealing to the tent,
Pulled down the crimson arras on the corse,
And in her mantle wrapt the brazen head,
And brought it with her ; and a great gong boomed
Twelve, as the women glided past the guard
With measured footstep : but outside the camp,
Terror seized on them, and they fled like wraiths
Through the hushed midnight into the black woods,

Where, from gnarled roots and ancient, palsied trees,
Dread shapes, upstarting, clutched at them ; and once
A nameless bird in branches overhead
Screeched, and the blood grew cold about their hearts.
By mouldy caves, the hooded viper's haunt,
Down perilous steeps, and through the desolate gorge,
Onward they flew, with madly streaming hair,
Bearing their hideous burden, till at last,
Wild with the pregnant horrors of the night,
They dashed themselves against the City's gate.

The hours dragged by, and in the Assur camp
The pulse of life was throbbing languidly,
When from the outer waste an Arab scout
Rushed pale and breathless on the morning watch,
With a strange story of a Head that hung
High in the air above the City's wall —
A livid Head, with knotted, snake-like curls —
And how the face was like a face he knew,
And how it turned and twisted in the wind,
And how it stared upon him with fixt orbs,
Till it was not in mortal man to stay ;
And how he fled, and how he thought the Thing
Came bowling through the wheat-fields after him.
And some that listened were appalled, and some
Derided him ; but not the less they threw
A furtive glance toward the shadowy wood.

Bagoas, among the idlers, heard the man,
And quick to bear the tidings to his lord,
Ran to the tent, and called, " My lord, awake !
Awake, my lord ! " and lingered for reply.

15

But answer came there none.   Again he called,
And all was still.   Then, laughing in his heart
To think how deeply Holofernes slept
Wrapt in soft arms, he lifted up the screen,
And marvelled, finding no one in the tent
Save Holofernes, buried to the waist,
Head foremost in the canopies.   He stoopt,
And drawing back the damask folds beheld
His master, the grim giant, lying dead.

As in some breathless wilderness at night
A leopard, pinioned by a falling tree,
Shrieks, and the echoes, mimicking the cry,
Repeat it in a thousand different keys
By lonely heights and unimagined caves,
So shrieked Bagoas, and so his cry was caught
And voiced along the vast Assyrian lines,
And buffeted among the hundred hills.
Then ceased the tumult sudden as it rose,
And a great silence fell upon the camps,
And all the people stood like blocks of stone
In some deserted quarry; then a voice
Blown through a trumpet clamored: *He is dead!
The Prince is dead!   The Hebrew witch hath slain
Prince Holofernes!   Fly, Assyrians, fly!*

As from its lair the mad tornado leaps,
And, seizing on the yellow desert sands,
Hurls them in swirling masses, cloud on cloud,
So, at the sounding of that baleful voice,
A panic seized the mighty Assur hosts,
And flung them from their places.

With wild shouts
Across the hills in pale dismay they fled,
Trampling the sick and wounded under foot,
Leaving their tents, their camels, and their arms,
Their horses, and their gilded chariots.
Then with a dull metallic clang the gates
Of Bethulîa opened, and from each
A sea of spears surged down the arid hills
And broke remorseless on the flying foe —
Now hemmed them in upon a river's bank,
Now drove them shrieking down a precipice,
Now in the mountain-passes slaughtered them,
Until the land, for many a weary league,
Was red, as in the sunset, with their blood.
And other cities, when they saw the rout
Of Holofernes, burst their gates, and joined
With trump and banner in the mad pursuit.
Three days before those unrelenting spears
The cohorts fled, but on the fourth they past
Beyond Damascus into their own land.

So, by God's grace and this one woman's hand,
The tombs and temples of the Just were saved;
And evermore throughout fair Israel
The name of Judith meant all noblest things
In thought and deed; and Judith's life was rich
With that content the world takes not away.
And far-off kings, enamoured of her fame,
Bluff princes, dwellers by the salt sea-sands,
Sent caskets most laboriously carved
Of ivory, and papyrus scrolls, whereon
Was writ their passion; then themselves did come

With spicy caravans, in purple state,
To seek regard from her imperial eyes.
But she remained unwed, and to the end
Walked with the angels in her widow's weeds.

V.

SONNETS.

SONNETS.

I.

MIRACLES.

SICK of myself and all that keeps the light
Of the blue skies away from me and mine,
I climb this ledge, and by this wind-swept pine
Lingering, watch the coming of the night.
'Tis ever a new wonder to my sight.
Men look to God for some mysterious sign,
For other stars than those that nightly shine,
For some unnatural symbol of His might: —
Wouldst see a miracle as grand as those
The prophets wrought of old in Palestine?
Come watch with me the shaft of fire that glows
In yonder West; the fair, frail palaces,
The fading alps and archipelagoes,
And great cloud-continents of sunset-seas.

FREDERICKSBURG.

THE increasing moonlight drifts across my bed,
And on the churchyard by the road, I know
It falls as white and noiselessly as snow. . . .
'T was such a night two weary summers fled :
The stars, as now, were waning overhead.
Listen ! Again the shrill-lipped bugles blow
Where the swift currents of the river flow
Past Fredericksburg: far off the heavens are red
With sudden conflagration: on yon height,
Linstock in hand, the gunners hold their breath :
A signal-rocket pierces the dense night,
Flings its spent stars upon the town beneath :
Hark ! — the artillery massing on the right,
Hark ! — the black squadrons wheeling down to
        Death !

PURSUIT AND POSSESSION.

WHEN I behold what pleasure is Pursuit,
What life, what glorious eagerness it is ;
Then mark how full Possession falls from this,
How fairer seems the blossom than the fruit —
I am perplext, and often stricken mute
Wondering which attained the higher bliss,
The wingéd insect, or the chrysalis
It thrust aside with unreluctant foot.
Spirit of verse, that still elud'st my art,
Thou airy phantom that dost ever haunt me,
O never, never rest upon my heart,
If when I have thee I shall little want thee !
Still flit away in moonlight, rain, and dew,
Will-of-the-wisp, that I may still pursue !

EGYPT.

FANTASTIC Sleep is busy with my eyes:
I seem in some waste solitude to stand
Once ruled of Cheops: upon either hand
A dark illimitable desert lies,
Sultry and still — a realm of mysteries ;
A wide-browed Sphinx, half buried in the sand,
With orbless sockets stares across the land,
The woefulest thing beneath these brooding skies,
Where all is woeful, weird-lit vacancy.
'T is neither midnight, twilight, nor moonrise.
Lo ! while I gaze, beyond the vast sand-sea
The nebulous clouds are downward slowly drawn,
And one bleared star, faint-glimmering like a bee,
Is shut in the rosy outstretched hand of Dawn.

EUTERPE.

Now if Euterpe held me not in scorn,
I 'd shape a lyric, perfect, fair, and round
As that thin band of gold wherewith I bound
Your slender finger our betrothal morn.
Not of Desire alone is music born,
Not till the Muse wills is our passion crowned:
Unsought she comes, if sought but seldom found.
Hence is it Poets often are forlorn,
Taciturn, shy, self-immolated, pale,
Taking no healthy pleasure in their kind —
Wrapt in their dream as in a coat-of-mail.
Hence is it I, the least, a very hind,
Have stolen away into this leafy vale
Drawn by the flutings of the silvery wind.

AT BAY RIDGE, LONG ISLAND.

PLEASANT it is to lie amid the grass
Under these shady locusts, half the day,
Watching the ships reflected on the Bay,
Topmast and shroud, as in a wizard's glass:
To see the happy-hearted martins pass,
Brushing the dew-drops from the lilac spray:
Or else to hang enamoured o'er some lay
Of fairy regions: or to muse, alas!
On Dante, exiled, journeying outworn:
On patient Milton's sorrowfulest eyes
Shut from the splendors of the Night and Morn :
To think that now, beneath the Italian skies,
In such clear air as this, by Tiber's wave,
Daisies are trembling over Keats's grave.

BY THE POTOMAC.

THE soft new grass is creeping o'er the graves
By the Potomac; and the crisp ground-flower
Lifts its blue cup to catch the passing shower;
The pine-cone ripens, and the long moss waves
Its tangled gonfalons above our braves.
Hark, what a burst of music from yon bower! —
The Southern nightingale that, hour by hour,
In its melodious summer madness raves.
Ah, with what delicate touches of her hand,
With what sweet voices, Nature seeks to screen
The awful Crime of this distracted land —
Sets her birds singing, while she spreads her green
Mantle of velvet where the Murdered lie,
As if to hide the horror from God's eye.

I.

ENAMORED ARCHITECT OF AIRY RHYME.

ENAMORED architect of airy rhyme,
Build as thou wilt; heed not what each man says.
Good souls, but innocent of dreamers' ways,
Will come, and marvel why thou wastest time:
Others, beholding how thy turrets climb
'Twixt theirs and heaven, will hate thee all their
   days;
But most beware of those who come to praise.
O Wondersmith, O worker in sublime
And heaven-sent dreams, let art be all in all;
Build as thou wilt, unspoiled by praise or blame,
Build as thou wilt, and as thy light is given:
Then, if at last the airy structure fall,
Dissolve, and vanish — take thyself no shame.
They fail, and they alone, who have not striven.

THREE FLOWERS.

TO BAYARD TAYLOR.

HEREWITH I send you three pressed withered flowers:
This one was white, with golden star; this, blue
As Capri's cave; that, purple and shot through
With sunset-orange. Where the Duomo towers
In diamond air, and under hanging bowers
The Arno glides, this faded violet grew
On Landor's grave; from Landor's heart it drew
Its magic azure in the long spring hours.
Within the shadow of the Pyramid
Of Caius Cestius was the daisy found,
White as the soul of Keats in Paradise.
The pansy — there were hundreds of them, hid
In the thick grass that folded Shelley's mound, .
Guarding his ashes with most lovely eyes.

AN ALPINE PICTURE.

STAND here and look, and softly hold your breath
Lest the vast avalanche come crashing down!
How many miles away is yonder town
Set flower-wise in the valley? Far beneath —
A scimitar half drawn from out its sheath —
The river curves through meadows newly mown;
The ancient water-courses are all strown
With drifts of snow, fantastic wreath on wreath;
And peak on peak against the turquoise-blue
The Alps like towering campanili stand,
Wondrous, with pinnacles of frozen rain,
Silvery, crystal, like the prism in hue.
O tell me, Love, if this be Switzerland —
Or is it but the frost-work on the pane?

TO L. T. IN FLORENCE.

You by the Arno shape your marble dream,
Under the cypress and the olive trees,
While I, this side the wild, wind-beaten seas,
Unrestful by the Charles's placid stream,
Long once again to catch the golden gleam
Of Brunelleschi's dome, and lounge at ease
In those pleached gardens and fair galleries.
And yet, perhaps, you envy me, and deem
My star the happier, since it holds me here.
Even so, one time, beneath the cypresses
My heart turned longingly across the sea,
Aching with love for thee, New England dear!
And I 'd have given all Titian's goddesses
For one poor cowslip or anemone.

ENGLAND.

WHILE men pay reverence to mighty things,
They must revere thee, thou blue-cinctured isle
Of England — not to-day, but this long while
In the front of nations, Mother of great kings,
Soldiers, and poets.   Round thee the Sea flings
His steel-bright arm, and shields thee from the guile
And hurt of France.   Secure, with august smile,
Thou sittest, and the East its tribute brings.
Some say thy old-time power is on the wane,
Thy moon of grandeur filled, contracts at length —
They see it darkening down from less to less.
Let but a hostile hand make threat again,
And they shall see thee in thy ancient strength,
Each iron sinew quivering, lioness!

THE LORELEI.

YONDER we see it from the steamer's deck,
The haunted Mountain of the Lorelei —
The o'erhanging crags sharp-cut against a sky
Clear as a sapphire without flaw or fleck.
'T was here the Siren lay in wait to wreck
The fisher-lad. At dusk, as he passed by,
Perchance he'd hear her tender amorous sigh,
And, seeing the wondrous whiteness of her neck,
Perchance would halt, and lean towards the shore;
Then she by that soft magic which she had
Would lure him, and in gossamers of her hair,
Gold upon gold, would wrap him o'er and o'er,
Wrap him, and sing to him, and set him mad,
Then drag him down to no man knoweth where.

VII.

BARBERRIES.

In scarlet clusters o'er the gray stone-wall
The barberries lean in thin autumnal air:
Just when the fields and garden-plots are bare,
And ere the green leaf takes the tint of fall,
They come, to make the eye a festival!
Along the road, for miles, their torches flare.
Ah, if your deep-sea coral were but rare
(The damask rose might envy it withal),
What bards had sung your praises long ago,
Called you fine names in honey-worded books —
The rosy tramps of turnpike and of lane,
September's blushes, Ceres' lips aglow,
Little Red-Ridinghoods, for your sweet looks! —
But your plebeian beauty is in vain.

HENRY HOWARD BROWNELL.

THEY never crowned him, never knew his worth,
But let him go unlaurelled to the grave :
Hereafter there are guerdons for the brave,
Roses for martyrs who wear thorns on earth,
Balms for bruised hearts that languish in the dearth
Of human love. So let the lilies wave
Above him, nameless. Little did he crave
Men's praises. Modestly, with kindly mirth,
Not sad nor bitter, he accepted fate —
Drank deep of life, knew books, and hearts of men,
Cities and camps, and war's immortal woe,
Yet bore through all (such virtue in him sate
His Spirit is not whiter now than then !)
A simple, loyal nature, pure as snow.

"EVEN THIS WILL PASS AWAY."

Touched with the delicate green of early May,
Or later, when the rose unveils her face,
The world hangs glittering in star-strown space,
Fresh as a jewel found but yesterday.
And yet 't is very old; what tongue may say
How old it is? Race follows upon race.
Forgetting and forgotten; in their place
Sink tower and temple; nothing long may stay.
We build on tombs, and live our day, and die;
From out our dust new towers and temples start;
Our very name becomes a mystery.
What cities no man ever heard of lie
Under the glacier, in the mountain's heart,
In violet glooms beneath the moaning sea!

X.

AT STRATFORD–UPON–AVON.

TO EDWIN BOOTH.

THUS spake his dust (so seemed it as I read
The words): *Good frend, for Jesvs' sake forbeare*
(Poor ghost!) *To digg the dvst enclosèd heare*—
Then came the malediction on the head
Of whoso dare disturb the sacred dead.
Outside the mavis whistled strong and clear,
And, touched with the sweet glamour of the year,
The winding Avon murmured in its bed.
But in the solemn Stratford church the air
Was chill and dank, and on the foot-worn tomb
The evening shadows deepened momently:
Then a great awe crept on me, standing there,
As if some speechless Presence in the gloom
Was hovering, and fain would speak with me.

THE RARITY OF GENIUS.

WHILE yet my lip was breathing youth's first breath,
Too young to feel the utmost of their spell
I saw Medea and Phædra in Rachel:
Later I saw the great Elizabeth.
Rachel, Ristori — we shall taste of death
Ere we meet spirits like these: in one age dwell
Not many such; a century may tell
Its hundred beads before it braid a wreath
For two so queenly foreheads. If it take
Æons to form a diamond, grain on grain,
Æons to crystallize its fire and dew —
By what slow processes must Nature make
Her Shakespeares and her Raffaels? Great the gain
If she spoil thousands making one or two.

SLEEP.

WHEN to soft Sleep we give ourselves away,
And in a dream as in a fairy bark
Drift on and on through the enchanted dark
To purple daybreak — little thought we pay
To that sweet bitter world we know by day.
We are clean quit of it, as is a lark
So high in heaven no human eye can mark
The thin swift pinion cleaving through the gray.
Till we awake ill fate can do no ill,
The resting heart shall not take up again
The heavy load that yet must make it bleed;
For this brief space the loud world's voice is still,
No faintest echo of it brings us pain.
How will it be when we shall sleep indeed?

www.ingramcontent.com/pod-product-compliance
Lightning Source LLC
Chambersburg PA
CBHW030801020726
47499CB00006B/1714